THE FIGHT FOR RISLANDIA

JON DEL ARROZ

ISBN: 978-1-951837-05-1

Cover design by Logotecture

Published in the United States of America

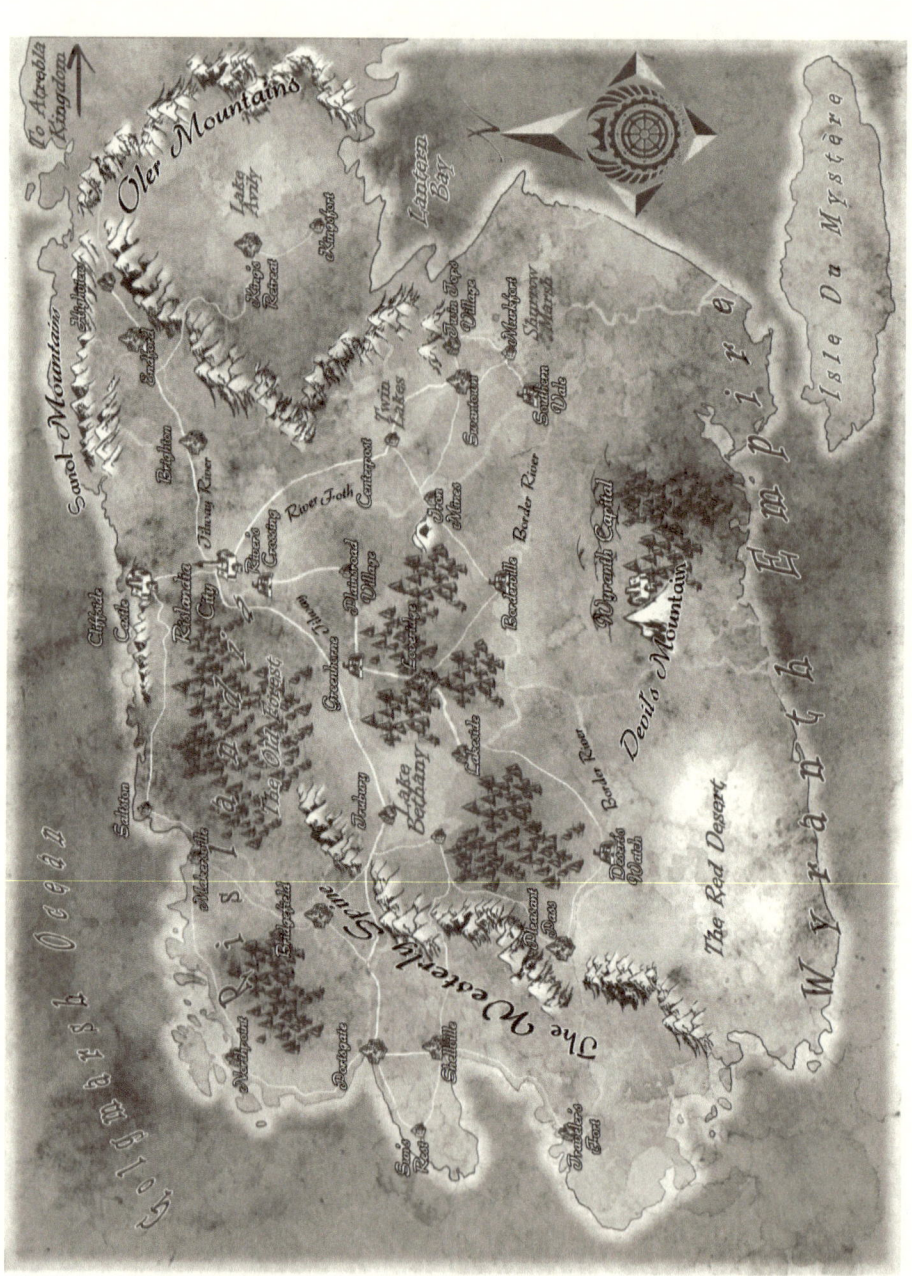

THE ADVENTURES OF **3** BARON VON MONOCLE

THE FIGHT FOR RISLANDIA

JON DEL ARROZ

CHAPTER I

I've been ordered to fly to Desert Watch. There has been reports of a Wyranth advance along the Border River. It'll be our job to slow them down. I hope this isn't the precursor to yet another deadly war.

An excerpt From Baron von Monocle's Log
Day 22 of the Month of Princes
24th Year of King Malaky XV's Reign

THE FULL MIGHT of the Wyranth army would be approaching the gates of Rislandia City within hours. Only one weapon could possibly slow them down, the airship *Liliana,* which towered before me. *My* ship.

We'd returned moments ago from a long mission across the Golgmarsh Ocean. Tired, injured, and ready for leave, another battle was the last thing my crew needed. But duty to our king and country doesn't tire, doesn't sleep, and couldn't fail now. This was the life we chose.

I glanced over my shoulder to see my father, General Theodore von Monocle, waving at me and smiling proudly. There was a sense of longing in his aged brown eyes, a look I understood well. He wished to fly with me, but he could not. I'd been named the captain of the airship, whereas he had command of the entirety of the Grand Rislandian Army.

Dr. du Clockhand descended the boarding ramp to exit the ship. A slim blonde woman in a laboratory coat, she had taken on the role of our ship's medic for our last mission. She pushed a cart of scientific instruments and beakers. Following behind her was Rhys, a strange scientist from the Zenwey continent, and Lieutenant Commander Marina Willet, a darker-haired woman in Grand Rislandian Army grays, one of my best friends. She hadn't donned her official uniform in a long time, and it was good to see her back in it.

The party stopped in front of me.

"Heading back aboard?" Marina asked.

"Yes, and you'll need to join me. The Wyranth are close and we need to fly," I said, motioning to another group of soldiers who came up behind me with crates of supplies and weaponry to restock the ships. "We're refueling and getting ready to go."

Dr. du Clockhand looked concerned. "So soon?" she asked. "What's going on, Zaira?"

"The enemy is marching toward the city now," I said.

Everyone fell silent.

"I believe it would be best for Dr. du Clockhand and me to head to her facilities within the city, with your permission," Rhys said. "We need to get to work producing a replicable cure for the Wyranth army's serum withdrawal madness."

"We shouldn't need a medic on our quick bombing run. I'll see you two soon," I said. "I should get back to the bridge and inform the others."

Rhys and Marina embraced, whispering in each other's ears. They were truly in love, and I envied how close they'd become. Would I ever have a relationship like they shared? If only I had the time or the ability to focus on anything but my own missions.

As if on cue for my thoughts, the two injured Knights of the Crystal Spire came down the ramp just as I returned to the ship. These were the two men who so maddeningly occupied my thoughts so much over the last several months. Why were men so difficult?

The first was James Gentry, a charming and strong farm boy with a pretty face. The taller, and more mature, Ethan von Lantern, followed behind him. Even though James had been my childhood friend, crush, someone I was supposed to marry, I found Ethan to be popping up in my head more and more lately. At least he'd been more attentive.

James had been distant lately. Ever since his parents died, really. Something in that moment changed our relationship forever, and I wished I could take it back, rescue them. If only for his sake. He'd never admit it bothered him, bottling up his feelings inside like he did, but to me, his unresolved pain was obvious.

James limped on a crutch and tread lightly on one leg, and Ethan had his arm in a sling. "Forgot something, Zair-bear?" James asked, a wry smile on his face as he teased me.

"No, heading back to battle," I said.

Ethan frowned. "I wish we could join you. We'll have to check in with Cid and the High Knight and report on this last mission."

"You need to rest up anyway." My eyes met Ethan's. In a flash, the world seemed to disappear around us. The way he looked at me... I can't remember anyone having looked at me that way before. I liked it. I *really* liked it.

James interrupted my reverie by snapping his fingers in front of my face. "Hey, lovebirds. You both have things you need to do."

Ethan flushed, running a hand through his short-trimmed brown hair. He laughed. "I don't know what I'd do if I didn't have James to remind me of my duties," he said, sarcasm dripping from his voice.

"Tell me about it," I said.

James grinned. "Here to help. C'mon, Ethan. Good luck, Zair-bear. You go kick the butts of those Wyranth goons all the way back across the Border River."

I let out a deep breath. James's lighthearted attitude managed to take the tension from most situations. It was an asset of his. "Thanks, James," I said.

I continued onto the ship, slipping past several men loading and unloading the various cargo crates and ship supplies. Marina came up behind me and appeared at my side. "Those are the new exploding shells," she said, pointing to a rack of oblong-shaped metal objects. Each one was about twice as big as my head. "Those should do a lot more damage than our old cannonballs."

"I hope so. We need to put a stop to these attacks," I said.

She placed a hand on my shoulder. "You'll do fine. You led us all the way across the ocean and fought off a whole army by yourself. We can deal with some Wyranth on the ground, no problem."

I hoped she was right, but we were tired, we were wounded, and hadn't had a break in weeks. Moreover, I'd spent weeks in captivity along with James, Ethan and Dr. du Clockhand. It'd be a while before the *Liliana* was up to full strength again, even if we loaded the cannons with new exploding shells. We watched as the crews completed their work, and Marina kept looking at me expectantly. What did she need from me? "Uh, did I forget something?" I asked.

Marina cleared her throat. "Permission to return to duty, Captain?"

I'd forgotten Marina had officially been a ward of Dr. du Clockhand on our last voyage, not a part of the crew, despite my already telling her to head back aboard. For more than two years, she had been one of the *Liliana's* cannoneers. She was probably itching to try out these new explosive shells our weapons specialists had made. After the losses incurred on our last journey, there would certainly be a place for her. It warmed me to think about having her back in action. "Yes, of course. I mean, permission granted, Lieutenant Commander Willet. Resume your station." I couldn't help but smile.

Marina saluted and departed through the cargo bay to the front stairwell.

One of the men loading cargo approached me and saluted. "Baron von Monocle, ma'am. I'm pleased to report the cargo is loaded and you should be ready to depart."

"Thank you." I returned the salute. "Let's close up the hatch and get flying."

"Aye-aye," the man said. "Good luck."

I turned to the back stairwell, closest to the bridge. After shuffling up the stairs and running into a few more crewman, I made it up top. The bridge was still in disarray from our last trip, with a blown-out window and one of the brass handrails dangling from where it had come loose. We'd reinforced the hull structure and repaired the punctures in the deck, but hadn't had time to get new glass. It would be a windy place for another flight.

Major Ral, our pilot, was dressed accordingly, with a big, fur-lined hooded jacket over his standard uniform. Lieutenant Colwell had the same, standing about a foot taller than the pilot and somewhat skinnier. Though it had been warmer on the Zenwey continent, we were in the dead of winter back in Rislandia. It would get very cold up in the sky.

"Do you have a coat, Baronette?" Lieutenant Colwell asked.

I shook my head. "I'll manage."

He shrugged. The crew had learned better than to argue with me. My blouse and corset were pretty thick, and with a velvet cape over them, it provided me enough warmth. Truth be told, I'd tended to get too hot during the course of battle, regardless of the weather. I thought about making a joke about men needing extra warmth while the women aboard didn't, but levity didn't seem appropriate given the situation. "The hatch is sealed. We're not going to get leave after all, in case you hadn't heard already," I said to the men.

"A courier came up and delivered the message," Major Ral said.

I nodded. "Good. Let's inform the rest of the crew and take off."

Colwell made his way over to our brass communications funnel and bent over to speak into it. "Attention, *Liliana* crew, this is the bridge. No doubt you've heard, but our leave has been canceled," he said.

A few groans came from the cracks in the floorboards between decks.

"There is a Wyranth force hours from invading Rislandia City. Brace yourselves for takeoff, and all crew to battle stations. Our mission is to slow their advance and turn enough of the Wyranth back for the city to remain safe. For steam and country!" Lieutenant Colwell shouted the last words with authority.

Echoes of, "For steam and country!" resounded from below decks.

The turbines whirred as the two big shafts on the deck started to spin, turning the propellers with them. The *Liliana* rumbled and began her ascent into the clouds.

CHAPTER 2

The mere sight of an airship inspires fear in our enemies! Oh, what a joy it is to be flying through the skies, and to have cannonballs to fire down below.

An excerpt From Baron von Monocle's Log
Day 25 of the Month of Princes
24th Year of King Malaky XV's Reign

IT ONLY TOOK us a few minutes at maximum speed to arrive at the foothills where the Wyranth Army was staging their infantry. On foot, it would have taken us several hours of travel. The Wyranth were positioned further south than when we'd first come from Portsgate to Rislandia City, just missing our path, or we would have seen them sooner.

Wind blew through our bridge's broken window, sending my hair into my face. I pushed it back to get a better look outside. A few dark specks appeared over the hills. I placed my eye to the lens of the embedded telescope in the command console, turning a crank to operate the other end at the bottom of the ship.

The specks came into focus. Thousands of soldiers marched, some on horseback, some carrying tents and supplies. Motored vehicles moved along with them, thick clouds of soot protruding from their smokestacks. They rolled slowly on treads beside their infantry counterparts. The vehicles pulled artillery weapons or siege engines in order to batter Rislandia City's walls.

"Bank us twenty-three degrees to port," I said.

Major Ral adjusted the piloting controls to turn the ship. Before our last voyage, he would have double-checked to make sure the course corrections I called out were accurate, but now he trusted me. It made me smile. I may get the hang of commanding an airship yet.

Lieutenant Colwell took his turn looking into the telescope. "That's one giant force," he said, pulling back to glance at me. "Should we focus our cannon fire on the artillery?"

I nodded. The Grand Rislandian Army could handle a mass of infantry, but their terrible weapons of war were another matter. Those had to be our primary targets. "Do it," I said.

He leaned over the brass communications funnel. "Cannoneers to the ready. Target the artillery on the ground, port side!"

I moved over to the port aperture, where the wind blew hard into the bridge. My eyes stung from the cool, dry air scouring them. But I didn't turn away. I had to see this. "It'll be a good test of our new munitions," I said.

"Oh yeah," Major Ral said. He stood on the tips of his toes to look over me and Lieutenant Colwell. "The courier mentioned we'd be receiving explosive shells."

Several members of the crew gathered around the port side railing to watch the cannoneers do their work. The hillsides below were covered in Wyranth soldiers. Leafless trees were scattered everywhere, and the grasses had turned a golden brown due to the season.

Several *kra-kooms* sounded from below decks. The *Liliana* lurched to the side. Major Ral frantically made some adjustments to steady our course.

Nine shells burst from our cannons toward the hillsides below. The Wyranth infantry fled as fast as they could, alerted to our position in the clouds by the noise of the cannons. With so many clustered, there would be little they could do to evade our assault.

Several fired guns from below, but standard rifles wouldn't do much to an airship this high.

Our shells hit the ground and exploded.

Dirt, debris, and pieces of the artillery shot into the air. Our cannoneers were incredibly accurate, most of the blasts hitting their main core of war machines. Several of their siege engines were blasted into bits. Their infantry scattered in every direction.

The *Liliana* passed over the marching Wyranth army and turned so the starboard side faced them. Our cannons fired again, the ship shaking as all the blasts fired at once. I rushed to the starboard side window.

More explosions hit the ground, swelling into a giant cloud of dust. I could hardly see anything as our ship circled around.

"Should we send in the commandos?" Lieutenant Colwell said.

"I don't think so," I said. "We should disrupt their forces as much as we can before engaging on that level." It wasn't a bad idea, though. If we could eventually capture one of the Wyranth soldiers, we might be able to get a better indication of their plans.

Lieutenant Colwell nodded. "You're right."

The ship kept circling. I watched down below, waiting for the dust to clear. A soft breeze blew the dust everywhere, but I saw a little of what was there. Where there had been motored vehicles, there were now only black ashes on the ground. These explosive shells did a lot of damage. "Wow," I said under my breath.

Major Ral looked over me. "You got that right. This ship just became that much more of a dangerous weapon."

"Incredible," Lieutenant Colwell said.

While we were distracted, something exploded near the ship. The *Liliana* shook. The sound was so loud that it made my ears ring. "Agh," I said, covering my ears with my hands. It didn't help matters much.

Something clanked against the ship and detonated. This one rocked us much more violently. I fell into Lieutenant Colwell, who held me up steady.

"They must have set up their anti-airship artillery," Lieutenant Colwell said. "We'll have to take those out quickly."

This would be the point in the battle where we would need the commandos to sabotage the enemy's firepower, but with so many of the Wyranth down there, and no Rislandian Grand Army forces to create a distraction for my small commando team, I didn't want to put them into undue danger. We would have to rely on our cannoneers for now.

I glanced out our broken window and saw the long barrels of the artillery placed atop treads for mobility. Steam puffed out the back of them as their engines maintained the power to fire shots high up into the sky. "Tell the cannoneers to target the artillery," I said.

"Aye, ma'am," Lieutenant Colwell said, moving to the communications funnel. He cupped a hand over it to speak clearly into it. "Anti-airship artillery! All cannoneers target and fire!"

Our starboard side launched another round of shots almost as soon as he had finished speaking. Major Ral twisted the *Liliana* around deftly, flying a more evasive pattern. Two more shots from the artillery exploded in the air where we had been just moments prior.

Our port side faced the Wyranth again and another series of blasts came from belowdecks. After the thundering of more explosions on the ground, no return fire came. The cannoneers cheered. They'd scored direct hits on the two weapons firing at us.

Major Ral took us further west, looping around the hills there before turning back. Some of the smoke had cleared. I looked to the ground. A handful of men scattered around where we had blasted. I didn't see any sign of vehicles or siege weaponry. We'd blasted them all to bits.

I couldn't help but smile. The city would be safe.

"Next time won't be so easy," Lieutenant Colwell said. "Now they know we have exploding shells as they do. They won't keep all of their machinery congregated into clusters anymore."

"Our cannoneers can handle it," I said, beaming with pride.

The major battle was over, but we still had more work to do. We could now try to capture one of the Wyranth like I'd hoped. Was this the way my father thought of situations as he came across them? Maybe command did run through my blood, just like the von Monocle luck the crew kept telling me I had.

"Major Ral, let's hover over by the forest area to the north. Now, we'll send the commandos down. Tell them to try to bring in a prisoner."

"Aye, Baronette!" Major Ral said, adjusting our course with the twist of a lever.

CHAPTER 3

Our commandos managed to tail some of the surviving Wyranth back to their greater army. What we'd found was only the beginning of their advance. We have to let our generals know so we can get the Grand Rislandian Army mobilized.

An excerpt From Baron von Monocle's Log
Day 29 of the Month of Princes
24th Year of King Malaky XV's Reign

I REALLY WANTED to go down with the commando team. On my last mission, I'd grown accustomed to tagging along with them, but on both occasions, it hadn't ended well. I was lucky to have gotten out alive.

Lieutenant Colwell watched me out of the corner of his eye, as if expecting me to make the proclamation I would be following the commandos dirt-side.

"I think it'd be best for me to monitor the action from the ship this time," I said. "There are too many Wyranth down there, and I would make too good of a hostage target."

A look of surprise crossed Lieutenant Colwell's face, followed by immense relief. "Very good, Baronette."

"Don't expect me to stay with the ship every time. This is an extraordinary situation," I said, making sure the point was clear.

"Of course, Baronette."

"Summon First Sergeant Wright," I said.

Lieutenant Colwell nodded and called Wright through the ship's communication funnel.

A few minutes later, Wright appeared on the bridge, saluting. He wore the darker shade of the Rislandian Grand Army grays our commandos sometimes donned, better for blending into nighttime or shaded scenery. Like all of the crew, a crest of Malaky adorned his right breast pocket: a crown, set into gears with wings on each side. Wright was a sturdy man, with a muscular upper body from years of descending the Liliana's rope ladders. His jet-black hair was covered by a helmet that matched his uniform.

"What can I do for you?" Wright asked.

"Assemble a team and drop into the forest below us. There should be Wyranth infantry scattered. I'd like to bring one in for questioning," I said.

"Easy enough," Wright said.

"Don't get too cocky," I said. "There are a lot more of them down there than there are of us."

"Aye, ma'am."

I nodded. "Very well, you're dismissed."

Those command phrases were foreign to me. It came out unnaturally, at least to my ears. The three men on the bridge didn't seem to notice, however. Or, at least, they were too polite to point it out.

Wright saluted one more time and turned to depart.

All we could do on the bridge from this point forward was wait. I walked to the window and then back again. Then, I did it at least a dozen more times while I waited. I could almost feel the rut my feet must have made in the wood from all of my pacing.

Sending our people into danger grated on me. I'd seen too much death already in my near-seventeen years. So many commandos were lost on our Zenwey mission, and several new commandos came aboard just before we departed. They hadn't even had time to get acclimated to working aboard an airship. But I couldn't worry about that. The Grand Rislandian Army trained our soldiers well. It was our chief advantage over the Wyranth, other than the airship itself.

Lieutenant Colwell stayed fixed on the telescope, watching the drop mission progress. We really needed two telescopes, or perhaps even three. Though Major Ral could get by without one. He kept his eyes ahead, focused and unmoving as stone. His sturdiness was what it took to be a pilot in combat.

"They've reached the surface," Lieutenant Colwell said. He turned back toward me, still bent over the instrument panel. "Would you like the view, Baronette? Must be strange not being down there with them."

"It is," I said. He understood what was running through my head. Everything he'd done for me since I'd come aboard this ship was a blessing. I couldn't ask for a better second-in-command. "And I'd appreciate a look."

Colwell stepped aside for me.

I moved forward and placed my eye to the telescope.

He had already focused the view for me. I could see the forest below. Dust floated through the air from the explosions minutes before, and the sun was starting to set across the land. Large trees cast long shadows, making it hard to see in some places. But there was enough light to make out my crew's location.

Wright's team had landed in a fairly concealed area. They fanned out, their guns trained around them. Wright moved through the center of the pack of six individuals as they quickly covered ground. I had to adjust the crank to move the telescope and keep them in view.

The crew disappeared into some trees. All was quiet on the forest floor, at least from what I could see. I wished we had a way to project sound from the surface so I could hear what was going on.

The moments dragged on into minutes as I worried about what was going on. What if my men had run into too many Wyranth to manage? They could all be dead. We could be sitting here idle while the Wyranth infantry reformed and progressed toward Rislandia City.

There was no way they could reorganize that quickly, could they? I couldn't imagine so many scattered people having that kind of discipline, even within the well-oiled machinery of a military. They had to still be disheveled.

"Anything?" Colwell asked, his voice betraying the same nervousness I felt.

"Nothing yet," I said. "I wonder where they went."

"I'm sure they're fine," Colwell said, more as if talking to himself than to me.

"Yeah."

More time passed. The whirr of our turbines became repetitive. It could take hours before the commandos would complete their mission. Riling ourselves up this early didn't do any good. My fear would rub off on the crew, as was evidenced by Colwell's reactions. I let out a deep breath and straightened, backing away from the telescope. "There's nothing to see for now."

"Mind if I..." Colwell motioned to the telescope.

"By all means."

He leaned over the device once more and peered through it. "No, you're right. Nothing to see. *Drat.* We can see most of our missions so clearly from this vantage."

He'd hit upon the cause of my nervousness in a nutshell. We could usually see everything from the airship, and here we were flying blind. It would happen from time to time, but it didn't feel right. Bombarding the big army had been much more satisfying, even if it was morbidly destructive.

Close to an hour later, a signal flare shot into the sky from deep into the forest. It sparked and crackled, impossible to miss, as it had grown darker out. "There they are," I said, pointing to where the flare had gone off.

"Adjusting our position," Major Ral said, not needing coordinates.

The *Liliana* turned slowly in place, and then proceeded straight to where the flare had been raised. Outside, our deckhands dropped rope ladders for the commando team, along with a harness to tie up any supplies or prisoners they might need to lift. I secured my top hat on my head and stepped onto the deck, cape flaring behind me.

The crew kept working, though some stopped to salute me. The commandos lifted themselves over the ship's railing as I approached. First Sergeant Wright was the last up, allowing his men to board before him. He saluted me. "Mission successful, ma'am. No casualties on our side. We managed to pick off a few of them, though."

After he spoke, the deckhands pulled up an unconscious Wyranth soldier. His uniform was nearly as dark as our commandos' uniforms, but he had a shiny silver helmet with a point atop it. The crew set him on the deck and removed his helmet. First Sergeant Wright stood by my side, towering over me. He reached into his pack and produced several vials, which he held out.

I took one of them. The vials contained a bright blue liquid, one I was very familiar with. "The giant's blood serum," I said.

"I assumed you'd be interested in seeing it."

"But they were out of their supply," I said, staring at the vial before clutching it. On my first mission with the *Liliana,* we'd uncovered a giant blob creature living at the base of a mountain in the Wyranth Empire. The creature was hooked up to machinery, which produced this serum from its blood, and the serum was used to create a stronger, more aggressive fighting force.

We'd bombed their facility sky-high. It had prompted the Iron Emperor of the Wyranth to visit me and plead for help. The serum was very addictive, and withdrawal made the soldiers erratic and mad. He'd told me he'd lost control of his troops, which was what sent us off to another continent to find a cure, in hopes of pacifying their rabid attacks. In theory, our mission should have benefited both sides of our conflict.

Except when I'd gone across the ocean, the Wyranth double-crossed us and invaded Rislandia. I'd thought the Iron Emperor had merely tricked me into taking our greatest weapon away from the fight, but perhaps there was more to the distraction. "He's found another supply," I said to myself.

"Hmm?" Wright cocked his head at me.

"Nothing," I said. I hadn't told the crew of my meeting with the emperor. They wouldn't understand, at best, and at worst, they could label me a traitor. It ate at my insides thinking about hiding the truth from them, but I couldn't let them know my decisions had been influenced by him. I should have known better.

The mission hadn't been a complete bust. We'd found a way to cure Marina from the terrible serum withdrawals. But this created far more complications than I'd thought it would.

"It makes sense as to why they're moving with such precision again," Wright said. "The prior border attacks were almost random, but these are precise strikes with purpose. This isn't good."

Several of the commandos picked up the unconscious Wyranth soldier and carried him away to lock him in one of our crew quarters. He could prove a valuable asset once he returned to consciousness. "Keep me updated as to his status. We should return to Rislandia City. My father will want to hear about these developments."

Wright nodded. "Very good, ma'am." He turned to assist his fellow commandos.

I made my way back to the bridge to order Major Ral to take us home. It would be nice to be back in the city again for more than a quick stop on the airship landing strip.

CHAPTER 4

As much as I would have liked to return north, our airship's presence here is more important. At least we can try to slow the Wyranth down.

An excerpt From Baron von Monocle's Log
Day 30 of the Month of Princes
24th Year of King Malaky XV's Reign

THE LIGHTS FROM the Crystal Spire illuminated the city. Though one could see the cobblestone streets clearly enough to pick out people and objects from my aerial vantage, the streets were mostly empty other than roving patrols of the Grand Rislandian Army. The king must have instituted a curfew or evacuated the city's residents during our mission.

I watched from the bridge as we landed. As usual, Major Ral set us down with minimal shaking, inclining his head toward Lieutenant Colwell, expectant of praise. Colwell patted him on the shoulder and walked past him. "I can't wait to get home to my family," he said.

"What about your favorite pilot family? Am I chopped liver?" Major Ral asked, feigning a frown.

"Eight out of ten landing. You rocked us forward slightly too much this time," Colwell said, exiting the bridge.

"No respect," Major Ral said.

"I thought you did great," I said, smiling at him.

"Well, you're the only one who counts. Hopefully, we get a few days' leave this time. You think the Wyranth will still attack the city?"

"I'd venture to guess we've set them back pretty good." I shrugged. "But we'll find out soon enough."

He motioned for me to go ahead of him, and I departed the bridge. After winding through the airship, I walked down the landing strip toward the castle. Even though it was fairly late in the evening, my father would want me to check in and report.

The commandos escorted their prisoner off the ship. They guided him ahead, toward our city's dungeon cells. It wouldn't be our job to interrogate him, thankfully, though I was curious to get information out of him.

The prisoner glanced at me, narrowing his eyes as he passed. "Holding me will do no good. You're all going to die the miserable deaths you deserve once the Iron Emperor's full plan is revealed. You have no chance!" He cackled.

His flippant attitude made my blood boil. It grated on me. I was too tired from the recent long mission, followed by having to immediately return to battle, to let his words go unchecked. Instead of letting him go to the dungeons like he should, I stomped over to him, catching up with the commandos. They stopped their progress when they saw me, allowing me to see the prisoner.

The man had long whiskers on his chin, thin-haired, not a full beard, and dirt caked on his face. He'd been in battle like the rest of us. His pupils were dilated, eyes filled with the rage only the Wyranth's serum could bring. It made their soldiers rabid, bloodthirsty, and this man was no exception as he bared his teeth like a ferocious animal.

"You're lucky you were captured by Rislandians and not by Wyranth. I've been in your jail cells and seen how your people treat prisoners. You should be treating us with respect. After all, we tore apart your army like it was nothing."

The Wyranth laughed. "It will only be a temporary setback."

19

"Why? What do you know?" I asked.

He merely grinned in response.

"You're going to talk one way or another. It might as well be now," I said.

The Wyranth dropped his smile and spat in my face.

I wiped it off, disgusted. The men holding him jerked his arms back, causing him some pain from the expression on his face. This whole interchange had been a waste of time. I'd let him get to me, and there was no good reason to be here. Someone would make him talk one way or another, but that someone wouldn't be me. "Take him away," I said through my teeth, motioning toward the city and the dungeon where he'd be held.

"Our empire is mightier than yours, and our scientists are smarter than yours. You have no idea what's in store. No idea!" He laughed like a madman again, and my commandos hauled him off.

The feel of his spittle still lingered on my face, despite my wiping it off. I wanted a shower, but it would be a while before I could get one.

While I collected myself, Marina appeared from the airship. She jogged to catch up. I slowed my pace to accommodate her. Under her arm was a little furred snout, sniffing around. Little feet pedaled in the air below her arm, trying to escape Marina's grip.

She carried my pet ferret, Toby.

"Thanks for grabbing him," I said.

"No problem," Marina said. She tried to set him down, but he leapt from her grip before being placed on the ground.

Toby scampered toward me as if his life depended on it. He jumped again, clinging to my skirts and climbing up me, as if I were a tree, before perching on my shoulder. Once there, he rubbed his wet little nose against my cheek.

I giggled. "I missed you too."

We continued down the landing strip in silence, both Marina and I tired from a hard day's work. Once we made our way through the city's side gate arches to the main path toward the palace, Marina frowned.

"You know, I never established a residence here. I'd only been in that institution. I don't even know where to find Rhys or where to go," she said.

"Why don't you stick with me," I said. "I have to report to the palace. Maybe we can get you some accommodations or find your boy."

Marina laughed. "He's hardly a boy."

"He's still a guy who decided to give up his entire life for you," I said. My words came out sounding a little envious, even though I didn't mean them that way at all. It was true, though. Rhys had gone from a powerful councilman among the Nightmen to live in our strange land, all for Marina. We wouldn't have even been able to escape without his help. I hoped he'd help find a cure for these Wyranth's serum addictions that we could mass disseminate. Even though we'd cured Marina, we had no way to make it work at a larger scale. If anyone could do it, though, it would be him. He alone had chemistry experience with the giant's blood.

Marina nodded in agreement and followed me into the palace. We found an attendant who led us around to the big war room where my father and Captain Talyen von Cravat spent their time planning the troop movements and logistics of the Grand Rislandian Army. Even at this hour, they were still talking with several of the troops, including an older man with white hair I recognized as the High Knight of Rislandia, leader of the Knights of the Crystal Spire. The knights were usually left to their own devices and served directly at the whim of the king. To bring them into army meetings must mean a dire situation.

I walked over to my father's desk where they were all gathered. We passed a scale model of the terrain, mapping out all of Rislandia and past the border river. It showed several Wyranth troop placements across our borders. It didn't look good at all. The expressions and tones of the people gathered with my father made the scene even grimmer.

"They have too many different fronts they're opening on us. It's like a trident with their initial force coming up the western coast, a group moving inland through the middle of the country, and another army coming up in the east. It must be the entirety of the Wyranth's forces. I've never seen so many troops on the move," my father said.

I approached, waiting for my father to finish speaking with the High Knight, and then saluted them.

"Zaira," my father said, nodding to me. "Welcome home. How did the mission go?"

"Well," I said, proud of what we'd accomplished. The long faces across from me dampened my mood, however. "It sounds like it wasn't enough, though."

My father's forehead wrinkled when he frowned, betraying his age. "No, it wasn't. You did buy the population of this city, and the rest of us, some time to prepare, however. The rest of the Wyranth are at least a few days' march from here."

"My crew desperately needs a break," I said, hoping I wasn't overstepping. "We've been through a number of extremely tough battles without stopping. They're spent."

He paced behind his desk. The others watched him intently. "War doesn't always allow for breaks. Your crew can rest up tonight, but I believe it's the best I can give."

I bit my lip but nodded. The crew would be none too happy about that, but they would understand. They had to. Our survival was at stake.

"When are the bulk of the Rislandian forces due to arrive?" the High Knight asked.

"Tomorrow," my father said. "We'll set up a good defense of the city and hope it will be enough. At least the bulk of the civilian population has been evacuated to Cliffside Castle." He moved to the model of Rislandia, tapping his finger down to the northeast of the country. "If necessary, we can fall back and make another stand there." He lifted his hand again and snapped his fingers. "Zaira."

"Yes?"

"I can't give you leave, but I can put the *Liliana* on a non-combat mission. The royal family will need to be escorted out of here. I haven't talked to King Malaky about this yet because he will fight me tooth and nail over it, but I want him and the princess to be safely in their retreat in the Oler Mountains by the time the Wyranth forces reach here. Taking them by airship would be the fastest way to accomplish it."

"We can do that," I said, glancing at the map. The Oler Mountains lined our border with the neighboring Atrebla Kingdom. They were much friendlier than the Wyranth, but outside of standard trade through boats and caravans, they mostly kept to themselves.

"They'll need Mr. du Gearsmith with them. If they need to flee to Atrebla, he has contacts there who can help keep King Malaky safe." My father's eyes scanned the model of Rislandia in front of him. "I don't know what we'll do if it comes to that."

"Let's worry about what we can do in the present, General," the High Knight said. The others didn't speak, but let the two leaders converse.

"Yes, you're right," my father said. "We can't get caught up in an endless spiral of doom, no matter how bleak it looks. I've been in worse spots before."

"Those exploding shells are very useful," I said, trying to lighten the mood. "We took out almost all of the Wyranth artillery we encountered."

My father forced a small smile. "That's good. We'll make use of our new weaponry again before this is through." He turned his attention to one of the other men present. "On that note, Lieutenant..."

The soldier stood at attention and saluted.

"Head to the weapons supply warehouse and ensure the *Liliana* is restocked. Even though she's going on a peaceful trip, she might not have time to replenish the munitions later."

"Aye, sir," the soldier said, turning tightly on his heels and departing.

I watched him until I felt a hand on my shoulder. My father stood before me, giving me a squeeze. "You're doing very well, Zaira. I'm proud of you. You don't need to worry about all of this, just do what you can. Rest up and be ready to go tomorrow. We'll take care of the rest."

I looked into his brown eyes, seeing the kindness, the love I'd wanted from him since I was a child. He was always away, always prioritizing his fight for the kingdom over us, but I understood his sense of duty now. It was an important part of my life. "Okay," I said in a near whisper, feeling like a child again beneath his intense gaze. The truth was, I did need to worry. My life, as well as everyone else's in the kingdom, depended on our next actions.

It reminded me of what the Iron Emperor had offered on both occasions when we met. It seemed absurd at the time, but he proposed peace in exchange for my hand in marriage. As disgusting as the idea sounded, would it have been so bad a sacrifice if I could stop all this bloodshed? I found myself shaking my head. Why was I even considering his absurd plan when he'd already proved so untrustworthy?

"It's okay, Zaira. We have von Monocle blood running through our veins. We'll come out of this alive and better than before," my father said, his lip ticking upward into a small, comforting smile. Though as much as his words were meant to be reassuring, he didn't quite sound as if he meant them.

"One more thing. Commander Willett," I said, motioning to Marina. "she needs some accommodations. Is there anywhere we can put her up for the night?"

"She can use the guest quarters here," my father said.

"Thanks. I hope you're right about our luck," I said before bidding everyone a good night and heading for my apartment.

CHAPTER 5

Desert's Watch is lost. We're managing an evacuation and retreat to Pleasant Pass. I have no idea what the Wyranth are up to, but we're badly outnumbered, even with having an airship.

An excerpt From Baron von Monocle's Log
Day 31 of the Month of Princes
24th Year of King Malaky XV's Reign

I MANAGED TO get a decent night's sleep in my apartment. As much as the place was technically my home, it had never felt so foreign to me. I barely recalled where I'd placed the furniture. When I woke in the middle of the night to use the bathroom, I bumped my knee twice—once against my dresser and again against the small table in my formal room. My leg had two distinct bruises the next morning, which I was careful not to touch.

Toby skittered onto my lap as I dressed for the day. I stopped and gave him a big hug. "At least you're with me to keep me warm, otherwise I might not have slept at all," I said.

My nerves were on edge ever since the prisoner had been so defiant right to my face. It might have only been the giant's blood serum coursing through his veins, but his distinct lack of fear made me very concerned. My father said there were still two more Wyranth armies on the way, and we hadn't completely eradicated the first, just slowed it down. And evacuating the civilian populations? It meant my father was seriously worried about losing the city. Everything I'd fought for these last months, down the drain.

But I still had a job to do.

Setting Toby down, I stood. Was I forgetting something? I gave one last glance around the small apartment. There wasn't much here to forget. My father's journals were aboard the *Liliana,* as were all of my logs and paperwork. This apartment was nothing but an empty shell. It felt very lonely in that moment, even with my ferret sniffing around the floor.

I opened my front door, allowing Toby to follow me. The first thing to do would be to head to the airship in case new orders had arrived. I wasn't the earliest of risers, which meant the crew would already be hard at work readying the ship for our next mission, whether that mission came today or tomorrow. I descended the stairs leading to the cobblestone streets of the city. A Grand Rislandian Army patrol of three men marched along, with a horseless carriage bringing up the rear. The carriage had a mounted gun with a long string of ammunition. Our people were ready for war.

The city's residents must have been so scared to see such militarization of their home. After evacuating, they must have been even more afraid. I imagined them being told they had to leave their homes and flee. In many ways, I sympathized. I'd had no choice but to leave my Plainsroad Village because of a Wyranth attack. I still remembered the clacking sound of the artillery advancing on my neighbor's farm, and Mr. And Mrs. Gentry panicking when they looked out the windows to see the soldiers advancing. The image of that evening clung vividly in my mind. It made me shiver now, exacerbated by a gust of cool winter wind flowing through the streets.

Leaves tumbled along the empty roads that had once been so full of life. It wasn't all that long of a walk, but I had to wait for Toby to catch up and to remind him to follow me. I wasn't about to leave him back in my apartment if we might have to leave the city at any given moment.

The little ferret had the shortest of attention spans. He veered off sniffing around at any given chance, which made me have to yell at him more.

We eventually made it to the airship landing strip, where crewmen loaded crates onto the *Liliana*. Despite some minor cosmetic wounds, the old ship wasn't in bad shape, considering she had just been on a voyage to another continent, fought off an entire force of strange bestial warriors, and then returned to another battle against the Wyranth. I smiled with pride at my ship's sturdiness.

"Ah, Baronette!" a familiar voice said. Harkerpal came bounding to my side, wearing loose, grease-stained clothing, not the standard uniform of most of our soldiers. He ran a hand through his black hair, his own smile flashing very white teeth that contrasted with his darker skin. "She's a beautiful ship, is she not?"

"I'm just glad I have you to hold her together," I said.

Harkerpal inclined his head. "Your father always used to tell me such things. The truth is, she's very well-constructed. I'm lucky to have been assigned to her all of these years. When I first came aboard, I'd known less about airship workings than even the most junior of my engineers." He chuckled. "My first week, I had an accident with the aether fuel which nearly set the entire engine compartment ablaze, while we were midair! You should have seen the look in your father's eyes when he came rushing into the compartment with a fire suppression unit."

"I'm sure it was amusing," I said. When I'd first met Harkerpal, his stories of the old days annoyed me, but now, I found them comforting. Something about being held captive without possibility of escape gives a new perspective on what to hold dear. I motioned him toward the ship and moved forward. "Come on, let's go have a look."

We entered through the main cargo bay and went our separate ways, as Harkerpal wanted to check on the engine room and I needed to speak with Lieutenant Colwell. I made my way through the ship up to the main deck, where Colwell stood outside the bridge, hands on his hips, watching the repairs of our broken window. Toby scampered along behind me before running across the deck and playing as if we weren't there. He felt at home here. So did I.

"Hey," I said, setting the tone for informality. It felt odd having military men like Colwell salute me. Outside of our missions where everything had to run like clockwork, I preferred to keep our relationships more casual.

"It's about time we had this thing fixed. Though glass windows will tend to break if we have more of these incidents. We managed to find some thicker glass this time. I hope it will hold," Colwell said, shaking his head. "You'd think with all the gadgets these scientists make, they'd be able to make something more break-proof."

"I'm sure they're working on it. It'll be nice to be able to talk on the bridge again without shouting over the wind... not to mention no longer having to deal with the wind blowing my hair around."

Colwell removed his Grand Rislandian Army hat, revealing a receding hairline with thinning hair. "I don't have that problem. Could always cut yours."

"Never!"

We both laughed. It was nice to be jovial, not to worry about being attacked or losing some of our friends for once. How long would it last? My laughter died off. "Have you heard anything about new orders yet?" I asked.

"While you slept two extra hours?"

"It's insubordination to mention such things," I said, feigning a serious tone and narrowing my eyes.

"My apologies, Baronette." He cleared his throat. "Yes, a messenger came from your father at sunrise. We're going to be taking off at midday, ferrying the king and his family to a safer location."

I nodded, recalling the conversation with my father. "I wish we had more time." I glanced over the railing. A group of people came toward the ship from the palace. Though they looked smaller from this vantage, I did see a glimmer of gold atop one of their heads—the king's crown. The royal family would be arriving sooner rather than later. "It looks like we're about to have some company. Come with me to greet them?"

"I'd rather stay here and, ah, supervise the work, if it's all the same to you."

Colwell hated pomp. So did I, but my misery craved company. "Fine, but you'll be responsible for Toby."

"Deal." Colwell grinned sheepishly.

I trudged back down to the bowels of the ship, reaching the ramp when King Malaky and his entourage arrived from the opposite side. With him was Matthias du Gearsmith, a gaunt, tall man who first introduced me to my airborne life. Behind them stood Princess Reina with my friend James Gentry lingering all too close to her side for propriety.

Reina wore an intricate dress of burgundy with gold trim, matching her flowing blonde hair, which fell perfectly over her chest. Her eyes sparkled with the picturesque beauty one would imagine from a princess. I caught James sneaking several glances in her direction. He walked with a slight limp but no longer carried the crutches from his leg wound. I wanted to smack him upside the head for looking at her the way he did.

Several other attendants reached the ramp to round out the king's entourage. The group was comprised of servants wearing the gaudy, goofy attire required of most civilians in the palace. Among them was one man I didn't expect, who wore subdued brown leather attire, someone I recognized instantly from his pronounced chin, brown eyes, and strikingly handsome face. Ethan von Lantern, journeyman knight. A man who had openly expressed interest in getting to know me better. Nothing like an airship mission to do that. My mouth went dry, and I struggled to breathe when he caught my eyes with his rock-solid seriousness.

"Zaira," King Malaky said, snapping me back to reality.

Startled, I jumped and then bowed deeply. "Your majesty," I said.

He waved away the formalities. "No need. These are dire circumstances and it's odd to see someone I think of as a niece giving me such honors," he said.

A niece? As I righted myself, I couldn't help but blink. I'd had no idea King Malaky had such affinity for me, even though he and my father were close.

Upon looking at him directly, I saw a man who hadn't shaved in a few days. He looked weary, despite his royal robes and crown. Several small white hairs sprinkled through his blond beard and glimmered in the sunlight, making him appear an elder statesman. He had bags under his eyes.

How much he must have been worrying for his kingdom. The news of the Wyranth invasion couldn't have sat well with him. But it was out of his control. My father and the remainder of the army were the only ones with the power to stop our enemies now. As heart-wrenching as it was for me, I could only imagine being in the king's position.

Princess Reina didn't look any worse for the wear. She whispered with James and giggled. A little anger flared inside of me again. I didn't like her, even though I knew it was just foolish jealousy. Why should her flirting with James bother me? She had every right.

James caught my glance and raised a brow but said nothing.

I cleared my throat. "Let's get you to your accommodations, your majesty," I said. "Perhaps you would like my captain's quarters for the journey? They're somewhat larger than the standard crew quarters and would be more comfortable."

"That would be lovely. It will only be a few hours by airship, however. I would like to at least watch the takeoff from the top deck if it's all the same to you. If we get tired of the view, I'll retire.

It's been far too long since I've been aboard the *Liliana*. I only wish this were under more cheerful circumstances."

Before we could move, a young private approached, wearing a Grand Rislandian Army uniform far too big for him. He saluted and his sleeve fell back along his arm. He must have been only fourteen or fifteen. I almost questioned how he made it into the army, but I recalled I wasn't all that much older than him.

I returned his salute.

The boy went wide-eyed at the presence of King Malaky, averting his eyes. "Ma'am, your majesty, uh... sorry to intrude."

"Go ahead," I said.

"General von Monocle wanted me to relay a message to you. He said his scouts have determined the Wyranth invasion forces are closer than expected. He recommends you leave immediately instead of at the scheduled hour."

That wasn't good at all. They were supposed to need a couple more days at the least to prepare for the invasion force. Fortunately, the civilians had already been evacuated. My shoulders tensed despite myself. "Thank you for the warning."

King Malaky frowned, bringing his hand to his forehead and rubbing it. "My place is with the people here."

Mr. du Gearsmith patted him on the shoulder. "Your majesty, we need to keep you safe. Once our army handles matters, your people will need a leader. Rislandia would be lost without you."

"I would be lost without Rislandia," King Malaky said, his face betraying his uncertainty.

His moment of vulnerability moved me. I'd always thought of the king as so stalwart, someone without emotions or real feelings. Now, he was as human as I was, and frail as well. These last few months, I'd questioned myself many times, whether I was worthy to be my father's daughter or if I could truly command an airship. All of those times I thought it was my youth or inexperience causing my doubt. But kings could feel the same turmoil as I could. I wished I had more time to reflect on it. "We need to get going. It will do no good if the airship is on the ground when the Wyranth arrive," I said.

"I suppose you're right," King Malaky said. He nodded resolutely. "Let's go."

The private saluted and departed.

"Close the hatch!" I said to the crewman at the mechanical control. He spun the crank, and the large door closed, sealing us inside the cargo bay. "Follow me," I said, leading my king and the others to the deck.

CHAPTER 6

Reinforcements have arrived at Pleasant Pass, including our sister airship, the Kerli. I pray it's enough.

An excerpt From Baron Von Monocle's Log
Day 33 of the Month of Princes
24th Year of King Malaky XV's Reign

THE *LILIANA* TOOK off toward the sky for the second time in as many days. Even though I'd spent the night in my apartment, I longed for more time dirt-side.

The royal contingent and their guards lingered out on the deck, including James, who had his arm linked with Princess Reina's. As we flew further from the ground, she gripped him more tightly. I couldn't help but shift my eyes to the side to watch a much more pleasing view of the shrinking city rooftops. I still couldn't get the image of the two of them out of my mind. It was burned there like a brand.

I should be happy for him. Jealousy was below me. It's not like I thought I could have a real relationship with James at this point. We could hardly talk anymore, let alone court each other.

"Are you alright?" Lieutenant Colwell asked, peering at me curiously. "You look like you're going to be motion sick."

"Yes, I'm fine," I said. His concern grated on me further, even though he meant the best by it. "I probably just need to get out to the deck and get some fresh air."

Returning my attention outside, I saw the king's entourage flailing in panic and shock. King Malaky and Princess Reina were prone on the deck. Guards covered them. Others took up positions around them, rifles drawn and pointed over the side.

What had happened in the few moments I'd looked away? "There's something wrong," I said.

Colwell turned to look. "By Malaky, what's going on?"

Both of us ran outside, leaving Major Ral alone to man the bridge. Several gunshots rang out. Some came from the deck, but others blasted from below us. With the enclosed bridge and the turbine engine noise, we weren't able to hear it from inside. Now I understood what had everyone so panicked.

I crouched, so as to not make myself a target, the rails blocking any view of me as I tried to figure out where the shots were coming from. Some of the king's guards and my commandos were positioned at the center railing, firing guns toward the city below. I crept toward them to get a better vantage.

Between the holes of the railing, I could make out figures on the rooftops below. They had rifles pointed at the airship. But how had they gotten there?

First Sergeant Wright appeared and crouched by my side. "It looks like we had a few Wyranth infiltrators within the city. They tried to assassinate King Malaky as we rose above the rooftops. They must have been delivering information on our defense and troop movements. No wonder they were able to advance so fast," he said.

Ethan had his gun drawn and fired over the railing. Once the ship lifted to a height where the bullets were unlikely to hit, he holstered his pistol at his side and turned to me. "I should have figured there'd be more. James uncovered a spy within the knights before we left for Zenwey. The Wyranth must have been planting their people for months."

I moved over to get a view of King Malaky and make sure he was safe. His guards surrounded him, but he looked no worse for the wear. Princess Reina appeared to be unscathed as well, dusting herself off.

"Whatever happened, it's too late to do much about it now," Wright said, his brow wrinkling into a frown.

"Perhaps we should send someone down to warn General von Monocle?" Lieutenant Colwell asked.

"A good idea," I said, "but with spies shooting from the rooftops, is there a safe place to set one of our men down?"

Before anyone could answer, an explosion rang out from the other side of the ship. Smoke billowed into the air. We passed directly over a building—or what had once been a building—that was blown to bits. The remains of it caught fire, and several of my people rushed to the other side of the deck to get a look. I followed, my heart racing. If Rislandia City wasn't safe, would there be anywhere that was?

"What happened?" I asked.

"A warehouse exploded. Can't tell much more than that from here," James said, hanging over the side.

Princess Reina pulled him back closer to herself. "Don't lean over like that. You're scaring me."

"It's fine, I've done it before," James said.

"Still..."

"I think we have more important things to worry about than James getting too close to the edge," I said, sounding a little too snippy, but Reina's doting wasn't helping me figure out what we should do.

"I agree," King Malaky said from behind me.

I nearly jumped at his deep voice, as if I'd done something wrong. I shouldn't have talked to the princess in that tone, perhaps, but the king didn't seem to mind. Turning to look at him, I saw intense focus in his eyes as he watched the wreckage. We passed the scene quickly as the ship moved forward. The bridge obscured some of the damage, but smoke still rose in the air over our rear tower.

"That's our primary weaponry creation facility," King Malaky said.

"What's that mean?" I asked.

"It's the place where our new explosive shells are fabricated. It means what we have on the ship will be the last of our supply," he said.

"If they're destroyed, at least they won't fall into enemy hands," I said.

The words only made King Malaky frown instead of assuaging him. Everyone fell silent for a long moment, sensing the king's despair. Weapons not falling into enemy hands still meant the enemy would be running rampant through Rislandia City, something we all would have considered unthinkable only a couple of days prior. I didn't have any idea how to lighten the mood or improve morale. Everything seemed to be spiraling like an airship about to crash.

"What about our cannonballs? Can we resupply those?" I asked, trying to change the subject to break the tension.

"We have storehouses for our more traditional weapons," King Malaky said. "Presuming the Wyranth haven't gotten to those."

I nodded, and then considered our current situation. "I think we have no choice. We have to get word of saboteurs and spies to our team below, even if it means risking one of our commandos. I'll need to head back to the bridge. Inform Major Ral," I said. "King Malaky, your majesty, I think it might be best if you go below decks for the rest of our journey. We don't want to risk any further incidents, even if we're high enough that it should be safe."

"I'm inclined to agree," Mr. du Gearsmith said from the assembled crowd of people.

King Malaky sighed. "Very well." He gave a longing glance back to Rislandia City as we floated further from it.

I nodded. The king and his entourage headed for the mess, and I returned to the bridge. Once we thought we were a safe distance from the city, Major Ral stopped the *Liliana*, hovering in place over a thinly-wooded area with tall grasses so a lone commando could descend and take a message back to the city.

I watched the horizon, hoping the Wyranth army wouldn't be so close yet as to destroy Rislandia City before we could return for its defense.

CHAPTER 7

The Wyranth have developed new weapons, mobile artillery we weren't prepared for. The Kerli is down and we are retreating. This doesn't bode well for the kingdom.

An excerpt From Baron Von Monocle's Log
Day 35 of the Month of Princes
24th Year of King Malaky XV's Reign

AFTER AN HOUR of flying away from the capital, my whole body was still tense due to my nerves. The bridge was quiet. None of us had anything to say, with the prospect looming of Rislandia City falling to the Wyranth. Such a heavy mood was oppressive. I needed a break, a cup of tea or something.

Back when I had lived a simple farming life, I didn't really drink much tea, but Ethan got me into the habit. It was a good one, too. Tea not only took the edge off my nerves, but the warmness of the liquid gave me a sense of comfort.

Now that I thought about it more, I found myself desperately wanting tea. I nodded to myself.

Lieutenant Colwell raised a brow. "Thinking again? It's dangerous when you do that," he quipped.

"I hope it's not more piloting thoughts," Major Ral said.

I crossed my arms over my chest in mock indignation. "You two serve at *my* whim, you know!"

"Yes, Captain," both men said.

We all laughed. "No, I'm going to leave the flying to you, Major Ral," I said. "My one experience crashing the ship was enough for me." Not that anyone would let me live it down. As much as the joking was a welcome break to the tension, it annoyed me that I still had to be teased about my one little mistake—okay, big mistake. At some point, I would learn how to pilot the ship again and I'd show them. But that day wouldn't be today. I uncrossed my arms. "No, I think I'm heading to the mess. Do you gentlemen have matters handled here?"

"Sure do," Major Ral said.

"It'll be another hour or two yet before we arrive at the Oler Mountains. And then we have to find somewhere to set the ship down, which won't be easy in that terrain," Lieutenant Colwell said.

"I'd like to see the princess try to slide down the drop ropes like one of our commandos personally," Major Ral said with amusement.

"You don't want the liability of that one," Lieutenant Colwell said.

"True."

I shook my head. "I'll leave you two to it then," I said before making my way outside. Several of the crew swabbed the deck. Others were in their lookout posts, and more had rifles trained on either side of the ship as a precautionary measure after what had happened on our departure from Rislandia City.

The king and his entourage had not come back out topside. As much as they wanted to see the views of Rislandia's open plains, they understood it would be better to keep safely below decks. With Wyranth operatives in the city, we couldn't take anything for granted with their safety, even while we traveled through the air.

As I walked the deck, I thought about the giants again. We had our hypothesis that there was another being used to produce the Wyranth's serum. After we dropped King Malaky and his people off, and did what we could to defend Rislandia City, I would pose to the crew that it should be our first priority to try to figure out where this new giant was located and cut the Wyranth off from their supply once more.

I couldn't help but look behind me, where Rislandia City was now far over the horizon, invisible except for a faint outline of the Crystal Spire. The bridge blocked most of the view. I couldn't help but sigh.

"Everything okay, Baronette?" a familiar feminine voice said.

I turned to see Marina. "You're above decks," I said, surprised she wasn't down in the cannoneer stations with the others.

"Nothing to do at the moment. Figured I would stretch my legs and get some fresh air," Marina said. "We have to take breaks in those cramped quarters, you know."

"True. I'm just worried about the city. What if they need us to defend them?" I asked, frowning.

"We're on orders to protect the king. We have to believe that our superiors have their priorities in order, yeah?"

She meant my father. Of course, he would do what it took to make sure Rislandia City was kept safe to the best of his abilities. But the way he had talked sounded as if he were almost sure we would lose it. I still hoped this was somehow a nightmare that I'd wake up from at any moment. "Yeah," I said, though I didn't come across as confident.

Marina clasped my shoulder. "Don't worry. With people like you inspiring the rest of us, the Wyranth will never keep Rislandia down. Military might can only do so much. You have to win hearts, and I know from experience, the Iron Emperor has no ability to do that."

"I know it, too."

Marina cocked her head at me with curiosity. "You do?"

I hadn't told anyone about my meetings with the Iron Emperor. James, Talyen, and my father knew a little about how he met me personally when I was trapped in his dungeon months ago, but I left out the specifics of much of our conversation. I told no one of the marriage proposal. It was too embarrassing to report. And for some reason, I was worried that knowledge of it would cause people to question my loyalty. It was a silly thing to fret about, but it lingered in the back of my head all the same.

But far worse was, no one knew the Iron Emperor had personally come to my apartment in Rislandia City. There was so much about that meeting I should have thought about, should have reported. The fact that he convinced me to take my airship to another land was bad enough. I should have known he had spies within the city if he could sneak about so easily. Someone had to be aiding him. Not mentioning our meeting to anyone was the most foolish thing I'd ever done, and yet, I still couldn't bring myself to talk about it.

"Did I say something to upset you?" Marina asked, snapping me back from my thoughts.

"No, I'm just frazzled right now. Chat later? I want to go get some tea from the mess."

"Sure. I'm always here to talk, you know. I owe you a lot... my life, really." She cast her eyes downward.

I smiled at her. "You don't owe me anything. I didn't do anything for you that you wouldn't have done for me." I tried to sound my most cheerful, even if it came off sounding a little contrived. "It's what friends are for, right?"

Marina's eyes met mine again, a glimmer of hope in them. "You're right. You always know what to say, Baronette. Go get your tea."

"Thanks," I said, walking toward the mess again. In truth, I was happy to extricate myself from the situation. It was hard to talk to people when I had secrets to conceal. It made me feel wrong inside, like I misled Marina somehow. I felt like the people closest to me understood I was acting strange, which only made matters worse. I really needed that tea to calm down.

No one else approached me as I crossed the deck, passing the twin turbines before reaching the door. A couple of the crew saluted me, and I returned the gesture lazily. I stopped in front of the door, breathed in the cool, fresh air through my nose, exhaling slowly from my mouth. Then I repeated the slow breaths several times. It was something Talyen taught me to calm myself. And it worked wonders. I would be ready to talk with anyone after a few more rounds of breathing.

With my resolve firm, I opened the door to the mess.

The area where the crew relaxed was mostly empty. Everyone was too tense and at their stations, other than those who were catching a breath of fresh air on the deck. It would be a good place to have some peace and quiet to myself. Except in the darkened corner of the room, I saw two figures close to each other. They didn't notice me at first, but as I stepped forward, and my eyes adjusted to less light, they became clearly visible: James and Princess Reina.

And they were kissing.

My stomach churned at the sight. As much as I wanted to look away, I found I couldn't. Their lips smacked together, further nauseating me. This was my ship. I wouldn't have this kind of untoward behavior going on. Not from James, especially. "James Allen Gentry, what by Malaky do you think you're doing?"

James jumped, slamming his back into the wall. "I..." He pinned his hands to his sides. "We were just talking."

I gave him a death glare.

Princess Reina turned around, her countenance expressionless, save for a small glimmer in her eye that I could swear was annoyance. Her upbringing had been far too political for her to show any shock or fear. "Hello, Zaira," she said.

She acted as if I'd stumbled upon nothing at all. The audacity of her! I didn't even know how to respond to her casual reaction to my walking in on them. Did she have no shame?

James said nothing, eyes shifting between the two of us. He knew better because I'd box his ears in if he acted up, princess present or not.

I shook my head at the sight of them. It was a farce, and I didn't have the time or energy to deal with this while having to juggle my responsibilities of commanding an airship. Both of them looked at me as if they expected me to say something. Instead of lecturing them, I spun on my heels and stormed back out onto the deck.

CHAPTER 8

We're having to evacuate civilians again, this time from Pleasant Pass. It's an administrative nightmare. This isn't what I signed up for when I agreed to be an airship adventurer.

An excerpt From Baron von Monocle's Log
Day 37 of the Month of Princes
24th Year of King Malaky XV's Reign

I HEADED BACK toward the bridge but paused to think. What was I doing? It wasn't as if I were unaware of James and Princess Reina getting closer. I'd been fretting about it every time I saw them together. But seeing such a public display... *I never!* I could hardly think any longer, which made the bridge the last place I should go.

Marina was no longer standing by the railing, which meant she'd gone back to her station. It was for the better. I didn't want to have to talk to anyone. I wanted to be alone. I wanted... What did I want?

"Zair-bear?"

I nearly jumped out of my skin at the voice. Only one person could have called me by that name. I turned. James stood before me. Reina peered from behind the door, trying to keep herself concealed.

James's face was covered in worry. He didn't want to upset me, but I didn't want to see him.

"I don't want to talk right now," I said, turning my head to the side.

James didn't listen. He never did. Attempting to bury my head in the proverbial sand would only make him dig in further. He shuffled to the side to reenter my field of vision. "Come on," he said.

I turned my head again.

He didn't give up but moved in front of me again, bending to the side to meet my eyes, almost daring me to move again.

I held firm this time, not one to back down from conflict. "Why is *she* watching us?" I asked.

James made a shooing motion to Reina, who closed the door of the mess. He turned back to me. "Better?"

I shrugged.

"Look, I don't even know what I did wrong. I don't understand girls!"

"No, you don't."

"Am I supposed to ask your permission to like someone? It's not like you asked me permission to be getting all close with Ethan."

"That's different," I said, unable to help but look away again. This time, I moved over to the ship's railing and leaned into it, watching as the *Liliana* floated past the land below.

James moved to my side, leaning over the railing as well. "How?"

"It just is. We weren't kissing, for one."

"Never?"

I scoffed and slapped him on the arm. "Never. And you shouldn't be asking a lady such things anyway."

James grinned wickedly. "I should be stealing such things."

"Not from me, you won't."

His amusement died as quickly as it crossed his face. "Seriously, I don't mean to hurt you, Zair-bear. I really thought... you know..." he scratched his head. "Why is this so tough to talk about?"

"I don't know." It *was* tough to talk about, though. I even hated thinking about it.

James stared over the side of the ship, wrinkling his brow as he collected his thoughts. "I seriously thought there was nothing between us. I know our mums used to joke about us marrying and combining farms one day, and the other adults in the village seemed to think it was a given, but since we left there, things changed."

"Yeah," I said, trying not to get choked up. Even though I knew better, it felt like he was being ripped from me. But that damage had been done long ago. We would never go back to the way we were, as much as I wanted it. Our lives were far too complicated now.

He turned to face me. "I love you. You know I do."

I bit my lip. Why did he have to say that now? I tried to fight tears from forming in my eyes, but it did no good. They came. "I love you too, James."

Then he grabbed me by the arms. "Like a sister."

It wasn't the first time he'd said those words, and it stung. And I knew I felt the same way toward him, like he was my brother. I had no compulsion to kiss him, even handsome as he was. We'd been too close over the years, for good and bad. We used to tease each other, fight like siblings, and we'd do anything for each other. There was nothing more through years of growing up together.

So, why did it hurt so badly?

I raised my hand to wipe a tear from my cheek, inadvertently causing his arm to fall to his side. Part of me wanted to bury my face into his shoulder and hug him, but if Reina saw that, it would only cause more problems. Even though she made me so angry, I didn't actually want to hurt his relationship with her. How many men had the opportunity to court a princess? I couldn't ruin it for him. "I'm sorry. I really don't know what I'm thinking."

"Me either," James said.

I took a deep breath to try to compose myself. "It's fine. You can do whatever with Princess Reina. Just be careful, okay? Public kissing, you could get into trouble. If King Malaky found out…"

"King Malaky found out what?" Another voice came from behind us. It was the king.

I froze.

James grabbed my arm and twirled me to face the king. "Hello, your majesty. Zaira was just worried about Rislandia City." His eyes shifted over to me and back again. "She doesn't want you worrying, too. She's very beside herself. Bad phrasing."

King Malaky surveyed me for a long moment, and then reached out his own hand to wipe the tears from my cheek. "There, there, Zaira. I understand exactly how you feel. Leaving the city is a burden on me like you might not be able to fathom. I live and breathe Rislandia City. As do you, I see. But you need not cry. We will prevail and restore our homeland. As long as I draw breath, I promise I will fight toward that end."

The king held such conviction in his words and in his expression that it filled my heart, just as it had been emptied a moment prior. My eyes stopped watering. "Yes, your majesty. Me as well."

He smiled at me. "I know you will. And you, too, James," he said.

"Thank you, your majesty," James said.

The king glanced around the deck, aloof. "Have either of you seen my daughter?"

"I believe she's in the mess," James said.

"Very well. I'll leave you two to it. Keep the faith!" King Malaky said, striding away with the confident pace only a king could muster. His velvet caped flowed behind him.

James drooped his shoulders. "That was close," he said when the king was out of earshot.

"We need to be quieter," I said. Unfortunately, it was tough to speak softly on the open deck with the intensity of the wind and the turbines whirring.

"So, where were we?" James asked.

47

"Us?" I said.

"Yeah."

A long silence lingered. All I wanted to do now was to go below decks and snuggle with my ferret. I didn't have to worry about any of this with Toby. He loved me unconditionally. As long as I fed him.

James sighed. "It's a relief to talk about this, really. I mean... not knowing. Now we know. Family, but not the husband and wife kind."

"Right."

"I'm fine with you and Ethan, you know. You'd make a good match. And he really likes you."

"I know." And it was eating me up inside. Almost like I was cheating on him emotionally. But I'd made no commitments. We hadn't even had a single date yet. All of this was so messy. Why couldn't feelings just be easy and make sense?

James looked at me expectantly.

I gulped. "I... I guess I give you permission to court Princess Reina. Not that you need it." Those words were so difficult to spit out, but they were necessary.

"Thank you, Zair-bear." He patted me on the shoulder. "This will all be for the best. It's good we worked this out now. With me guarding the royal family and you off on this ship, who knows what can happen? If something was left unsaid, if we didn't know..." He shook his head.

"Let's not think about that," I said. It was hard enough as it was.

"You're right. Sorry to make you cry."

"It's okay."

James nodded. Another awkward silence fell between us. He forced a smile. "I'll leave you be then. Don't be a stranger, okay? We should talk like we used to sometime."

"Yeah."

James walked away, and I watched after him as he entered the mess before turning back to the view of the land below. We crossed over a hilly area. The Oler Mountains wouldn't be far. It would mean the end of our journey.

I was freed from any personal burdens I had when we started our flight. James and I could be friends, and now it was clear, without either of us having to worry about each other's feelings. But why did I feel more alone than ever before?

The wind picked up, and I wrapped my hands around myself to fight the chill of the cold air.

CHAPTER 9

We landed just outside of Lake Bethany, where we are directing the citizens of Pleasant Pass to come while we work through this mess of a situation. It's a beautiful place. I hope the Wyranth never make it this far into our kingdom.

An excerpt From Baron Von Monocle's Log
Day 40 of the Month of Princes
24th Year of King Malaky XV's Reign

MAJOR RAL FOUND a place to land the ship on a flat area in the bowl surrounded by mountains. Lake Avily was close, a peaceful and serene place. A village cropped up right by the lake, which was where King Malaky and his retinue would make their accommodations. With the amount of mountainous terrain here, and a good portion of the Grand Rislandian Army stationed further south, it would be difficult for the Wyranth to make it to this location without giving enough warning to the royal family that they could flee into Atrebla. That was the hope, at least.

I forced myself to head to the cargo bay where the king's entourage would be departing. Ever since seeing James and Princess Reina together, I hadn't wanted to be near them. It would be awkward at best, even with the new understanding James and I had.

King Malaky shook hands with the crew, thanking them for their service, and judging by the looks in their eyes, instilling in them a renewed resolve to fight. Most of the crew had assembled to watch their king depart, and soon, he was near the exit, facing us, with all eyes on him. He scanned the crowd, inclining his head.

"To serve on the *Liliana* is one of the greatest honors Rislandia has to offer, and you all have done a marvelous job in representing our people." He paused to meet the eyes of several in the crowd, connecting with them. It was a trick to keep attention I would have to try on the crew sometime. "I'm going to be forthright with you. These coming days are going to be some of the most difficult in Rislandian history. We've already endured tragic losses: friends, family, loved ones. The destruction the Wyranth have wrought across our countryside has been great, but we have no time to mourn. You are the ones who will save our country and return us to the prosperous place we hold so dear. I am counting on each of you personally and want you to know that the hope of my heart goes with you."

There was a long pause before several of the crew clapped. It started slowly, tepid. Even with King Malaky's deep voice and refined words, he didn't promise victory for the crew. They needed more hope. I could see that. I stepped forward. "Don't worry, your majesty. You can count on us. We'll fight for Rislandia—and win! For steam and country!"

"For steam and country!" shouted my crew, raising fists in the air. Then the claps came in earnest.

King Malaky clasped me on the shoulder, smiling. "You're good at stirring a crowd, just like your father. I'll remember that in the future," he said.

My face became hot. The praise from the king felt good, I had to admit. "Thanks," I said meekly.

"I meant it that we're counting on you. Please, do all you can. And make sure your father doesn't go too far in his bravado. I need his strategic thinking more than he needs to run off into a group of Wyranth and get himself killed," King Malaky said.

"I'll do what I can," I said. If my father wanted to do something, it wasn't as if I'd be able to stop him. He was a force of nature at times. But I didn't want to lose him again if I could help it. Moreover, he had a baby on the way. He shouldn't be putting himself at risk.

"I know you will. Goodbye for now, Zaira. I hope to see you again soon." He motioned to his entourage, and they all turned toward the ramp.

Mr. du Gearsmith secured his top hat and stopped before me. "I daresay, Ms. von Monocle, you have matured considerably in the last several months. I am quite impressed."

"Thank you," I said. Was everyone going to shower me with praise? It was starting to feel awkward, especially with the crew looking on.

"Very good," Mr. Du Gearsmith said. He gave me a quick nod and followed the others.

My gaze drifted toward the ramp, watching so many people depart from the ship. My eyes caught James, who walked alongside Princess Reina. King Malaky noticed him, as well, and stopped mid-stride. "Mr. Gentry, aren't you returning with the *Liliana?*" the king asked.

"Ahh..." James said, eyes shifting to the princess.

"I've requested him as my personal guard," Princess Reina said, inclining her head. Her words sounded rehearsed. "He's done such a good job of defending our country, I feel safer around him."

King Malaky gave a very dubious look to the both of them, and then shook his head. "We don't have time to hold up this airship. Let's go." He stomped down the ramp.

Princess Reina started to follow, but James held where he was, confused. "He didn't say I could come," James said.

"He didn't say you couldn't, now come on. That's a royal order, apprentice knight!" Princess Reina said. She had a wry grin on her face. She walked up the ramp toward him, took his arm, and tugged him away with her. James looked back at me briefly, but followed the princess.

It must be nice to be able to get whatever you wanted on a whim. I found myself becoming jealous again and shook my head. This couldn't distract me. I had an airship to run and a very dangerous mission coming up. My focus had to change. I turned back to my crew.

"Alright, everyone. Back to stations. We don't know what we're going to find when we get back to Rislandia City. What we saw when we left didn't bode well. Wright, Colwell, von Lantern, and Willet, meet me in the mess so we can strategize."

I clapped my hands together, and the crew disbursed, returning to their duties. After the crowd thinned out, I made my way through the ship, taking the opposite-side stairs this time, which opened directly into the mess. The others were ahead of me, but I caught up on the way. Ethan held the door to the mess open for me.

His eyes twinkled as I passed him. Why was I jealous of Princess Reina again? I had a dreamy man all to myself right here.

Once we'd all made our way inside, my people settled around one of the long tables. All eyes fell to me expectantly.

"I think we should prepare what we're going to do. I don't want to be blindsided," I said, not taking any time for niceties.

"A good idea," Lieutenant Colwell said, "but what can we expect?"

"Well," I said, "we know Wyranth spies are among our population, at the very least. They probably were sent to provide intelligence and soften up some of our defenses. We can only hope our scout made it to my father in time to deliver the message. If he did, odds of the city being secure from the inside are good. If he didn't..." I shook my head. The more I thought about spies being among us, it made me realize no one was safe. Not even on the airship.

"So, either way, our focus should be on the outskirts of the city," Marina said. "We can, at the very least, do a cannon run on the approaching Wyranth, like we did with the last force."

I nodded. "I figured we'd start there."

First Sergeant Wright cleared his throat. "We may want to do a drop of some of our commandos inside the city first, just in case. If there are Wyranth spies about, we can assist the city's defenses better, since our people are better suited to moving in a stealthy capacity. The Wyranth will notice our guard patrols, but we might give them an edge."

"Good point," I said. "All in agreement?"

Mutters of assent came from around the table.

"Okay," I said and exhaled deeply. This battle wasn't just another one to go fight. We'd faced difficult odds before, but this time, we had so much more at stake. It was like a giant weight had been set on my shoulders.

Giant. I'd almost forgotten.

"There's another giant somewhere out there, fueling these Wyranth. Let's not forget that. If we get a chance, we need to find out where it's located and cut off their serum supply. It might not turn the tide of the battle right now, but it'll make a difference in the long run."

"That's the most important thing we could do," Marina said. "Trust me, when you've got withdrawal from that stuff, it's impossible to focus. The Wyranth will lose all of their cohesion if we take away their supply." She knew better than any one of us just how potent the giant's blood serum could be.

I clasped my hands in front of me. "Right. So let's do this. We'll set down outside the city and worry about tackling a giant later. And try to keep positive. The crew looks to us for inspiration," I said.

Everyone stood, understanding they were dismissed. I watched them leave. These were my most trusted, the people I could count on. I hoped they would be enough to make a difference in the coming days.

CHAPTER 10

For now, the Wyranth seem to have slowed their advance.
We are finally returning to Rislandia City to bring news of
their aggression and of their new anti-airship weaponry.

An excerpt From Baron von Monocle's Log
Day 1 of the Month of Princesses
24th Year of King Malaky XV's Reign

"RISLANDIA CITY AHEAD!" one of my crewmen called from the deck.

The shout snapped me out of a mid-afternoon daydream. Maybe daydream wasn't the right word, but I'd been staring at the console in front of me for a long time, in an almost sleeping state. My shoulders were tight, my stomach twisted and knotted. Daydreams were supposed to be about hope for the future, right? All of my thoughts and imagination focused on the pending destruction of Rislandia.

Lieutenant Colwell stood hunched over the telescope. "Hmm," he said.

"What's that supposed to mean?" I asked.

"I can't see anything useful yet. The northern city wall and buildings are in the way. We're coming in from the wrong angle," he said.

"We can't come in from the other side. You know the Wyranth will be ready for us with anti-airship artillery if they're out there," Major Ral said, keeping his hands on the piloting controls.

"It's okay. Ease us in," I said, trying to get a good look out the bridge's port-side window. Countryside was all around us, broken up by a long river originating in a lake northwest of Rislandia City. It made the northern edge of the city more defensible, as it needed a bridge to cross, but those features didn't help in this instance. Black smoke rose in the distance, beyond the city. "That can't be good," I said to myself.

"Looks like an explosion," Lieutenant Colwell said.

From the deck, First Sergeant Wright made a few hand gestures toward the bridge.

"Oh, right. We need to drop our commando teams before we get too close," I said. I'd nearly forgotten the plan! The stress was getting to me. "Slow us to a hover, Major Ral."

"Aye, aye," Major Ral said.

The turbine's propeller blades turned to halt our momentum, rotating to a vertical position to allow the ship to hover in place. I motioned to Wright to give him the go-ahead. Several of his commandos stood to each side of the ship, holding the long ropes that would take them down. My deckhands had the ropes looped around spools with cranks so we could lower our crew slowly enough to avoid risking any injuries with the fall.

The first group of commandos jumped overboard, rappelling down the sides of the ship. They would flip around mid-drop, as I'd seen them do so many times before. They moved with such a synchronization that it made for an incredible sight. No one had quite the training like the *Liliana's* commandos. The Grand Rislandian army gave us their best, for which I was thankful. Pride filled my insides with warmth as I watched them.

Sergeant Wright was the last to the ropes. After he had monitored all of his men, he gave a salute in the direction of the bridge and rappelled over the side himself.

"Stay safe," I said, even though he wouldn't be able to hear me.

We waited several long minutes for the commando team to complete their drop to the ground before recalling the ropes. It would soon be our turn to enter into battle. The Wyranth were attacking, judging by the growing cloud of black smoke on the opposite side of the city. At the very least, we should be able to use the airship to slow them down. But we also had to get into the city and make sure my father and Talyen were safe.

"Loop around to the city's southern gate," I told Major Ral. "Take a westerly route. We might surprise the Wyranth if we come from that direction." It was a long shot that it would give us any cover. The airship's shadow was hard enough to miss, but we needed any edge we could get, no matter how small.

Major Ral said nothing but banked the ship and moved us forward. The Crystal Spire seemed to watch us as we made our way around the city, a fixed monument jutting into the sky, almost as high as we were. We were running somewhat low to drop the commandos and would need to stay at a lower altitude for the sake of our cannoneers' accuracy.

Even though we moved at a rapid speed, the airship's movements seemed slow. We edged around the city's gates. Lieutenant Colwell finally pulled back from the telescope. "By Malaky," he said under his breath.

"What?" I asked.

"You should look for yourself."

I stepped over to peer into the telescope. Smoke clouded my view at first. An explosion *boomed* ahead, creating a flash in the telescope. It was loud enough to be heard this far up in the air. When the smoke cleared away, the view shook me to my core. At the southern gate marched the largest army I had ever seen. There were thousands of them, all in the same dark uniforms with metal helmets that twinkled as the sunlight reflected off of them. The Wyranth were here. And though we'd taken out one of their force's artillery and some other machines of war, they had dozens more assembled now. My heart seemed to push up into my throat. "This isn't good. We have to slow them down as best we can," I said. "Tell the cannoneers to ready their shots and aim for their artillery."

As if responding to my orders, something *boomed* much closer to us. An explosion triggered in the sky, rattling the windows around us. The Wyranth must have spotted the *Liliana* and set their anti-airship weapons on us. We had to act fast. "Evasive maneuvers, Major Ral!"

"Working on it," Ral said, banking us to the side again."

Colwell moved to the communications funnel. "Cannoneers, target their artillery and fire!"

They didn't need the prompting. Several blasts came from our port side cannons. The force of the blast shifted the ship and caused me to lose my footing. I slid toward Ral, who released the piloting controls and caught me in his arms.

"Oh my," I said, trying to right myself.

Ral didn't even take a moment to look after me but pushed me away, allowing him to regain control of the levers. The ship's nose turned down, and he dropped us a few feet. It was good he did, as another volley of explosives detonated where we had been a moment prior. Shrapnel fell on top of the bridge, pattering against the roof, harmless.

"Deft maneuvering, Major," Colwell said.

"Thank you," Ral said, but he was too focused to smile, sucking in his bottom lip as he turned the ship once more.

As the ship came about, the starboard side cannons fired. I managed to stand on my toes and get a look over the side. There were so many Wyranth targets, we couldn't help but hit and make a dent in their ranks. Our explosive shells did a lot more damage than our old cannonballs would have.

Plumes of debris lifted from the ground. The Wyranth cleared away from each of those blasts. But there were so many of them, they filled in the holes in their ranks within moments. There still appeared to be a lot of functioning weaponry down there. We needed something stronger.

"I wish we had one of those big bombs we dropped on the Wyranth mountain," I said.

Lieutenant Colwell frowned. "And the weapons facility was destroyed. But it can't have been our only one, can it?"

"I don't know," I said, "but my father would." The gears started turning in my head.

"I don't like that look," Lieutenant Colwell said. "You aren't thinking of going down there, in the middle of this?"

"We'd have to at some point anyway. Besides, I should be safe if you drop me far enough back in the city that it's behind our ranks."

"But not for long while the Wyranth are about to break through the city gates!"

As if on cue, something exploded below. The Wyranth cheered, which didn't bode well for us. I glanced out the window again. The city walls had been broken through. Our ship turned again, and our cannoneers fired directly into where the Wyranth would have advanced. When that payload exploded, smoke was everywhere, making it difficult to see. Major Ral spun us around again for the opposite side cannons to fire their second volley.

"We have no choice," I said. If there was an extra big bomb in one of the remaining stores, we might be able to use it to save the city. I was determined to make this work and win this battle. "One more round of shots and let's pull back into the city. I'll drop down with Marina and Ethan. We'll be alright."

"I really hate that you do this," Colwell said. "I thought you'd learned when you stayed on the ship last time."

"I know," I said, but my resolve was firm. This time, I had to do my part to change the course of this battle. "Call Marina and Ethan to the deck."

Despite his misgivings, Colwell followed my orders. Ral brought the ship in a loop around for another pass. The Wyranth spotted us this time, with three blasts resounding in the air nearby. One of those blasts came all too close to the ship. Our side railing cracked on the port side, splintering into thousands of pieces. It blew a hole clear through the deck on the outer edge. My people outside scrambled but, thankfully, no one was hurt.

Before I could think to react, our cannons fired again, forcing me to grab onto the railing to keep my balance. Ral kept the ship turning so the other side could get their last volley in. No more blasts came in our direction. Our cannoneers had hit the artillery below, but as I watched, something much more disturbing occurred.

Wyranth soldiers flooded through the gaping hole where the city's front gates had once been.

CHAPTER II

King Malaky is sending the full might of the Grand Rislandian Army to Lake Bethany, along with a contingent of knights, whose sole purpose is to destroy the Wyranth artillery. It's my hope we can make the skies safe to fly once more.

An excerpt From Baron von Monocle's Log
Day 3 of the Month of Princesses
24th Year of King Malaky XV's Reign

THE SHIP REVERSED course, the late-afternoon sun casting shadows across everything below. I stepped out onto the deck, leaving my top hat behind on the bridge. As much as it was a signature von Monocle look to have the hat, it didn't work well with longer hair. My father might be disappointed in my removing it, but I had to be efficient in everything, including how I dressed. I made sure my pistol was secure in its holster and my sword in its scabbard on the opposite side. Satisfied I was ready to descend into the city, I nodded to myself. "Prepare the ropes for a drop," I said to a deckhand.

"Aye, Baronette," he said and set himself to the task.

"And grab a thicker hauling rope for the return trip," I added. "We might need to bring up something big."

By the time the deckhands were ready with the ropes, Ethan and Marina arrived.

"We're not going to land?" Ethan asked.

"Too risky, I think. I don't know if you saw, but the Wyranth army have made it into the city. If we landed the ship, they might try to seize her."

"It'll be dangerous dropping down there, too," Ethan said.

"I know," I said, looking into his gorgeous brown eyes. They were filled with concern for me. I wanted nothing more than to gaze at him forever, but I had to stay focused. "Nothing's safe in war. We must do our duties."

"Are you two going to be staring at each other the whole time we're down there?" Marina asked.

Ethan turned a bright red as he shyly glanced away from me. I felt my face become warm, as well, but I wouldn't dignify Marina with a response. "The rope ladders, please," I said loud enough for the deckhands to hear. "I'm not going to rappel down like the commandos."

I'd used the rappelling ropes one time before, tied to one and foisted up to the ship when I was bleeding from a gunshot wound. Though they gave my commandos the speed they needed, I wasn't comfortable using them to slide to the ground. I preferred the rope ladders so I could have a sturdier footing. Even if they flapped in the wind, the ladders weren't all that bad.

My people dropped three ladders over the side. Ethan, Marina, and I each moved to our own so we could hit the ground faster. I didn't know what to expect when we arrived. How far had the Wyranth pushed into the city? We were positioned along the northern wall, and they were coming in through the south. The Grand Rislandian Army would meet them and slow their progress, at the very least, but there could be spies from before, or stragglers. I had to be ready for anything.

I flung my leg over the rail and caught one of the rungs below my foot. Then I lifted my other leg over the side. A deckhand kept hold of my arms until I was secure. I nodded to him that I was ready, and he stepped back. As I descended the ladder, I didn't look down. It was already frightening enough, wobbling through the air, knowing how high I was. Looking down would have paralyzed me. And so I kept faced forward.

Poor Toby must have been so worried, locked in my cabin. I laughed to myself. How absurd a thought. I was about to enter a war zone and my thoughts drifted there? But I cared about my ferret, and I hadn't much paid attention to him since I came aboard the ship. What if something happened below and I didn't return? I could only hope the crew would remember to feed him.

Descending past the bottom of the hull, I shook my head. I couldn't think negative thoughts. That wasn't how to win battles. It wasn't the von Monocle way, either. Part of me had trouble believing my father had gotten himself out of all sorts of jams simply by positive thinking, but the crew often maintained it was his secret formula to success. *We will win this. We will save Rislandia,* I thought firmly to myself. It couldn't hurt to try to be optimistic.

The *crack* of a gunshot resounded. It came from much closer than the raging battle at the gates of the city.

Something tugged at my cape. I couldn't help but glance over my shoulder as it flapped in the wind behind me. There was a fresh hole, ripped right through the bottom. *Oh, no.*

"Scoot down!" Ethan's voice came from behind me.

I shuffled down a few more rungs. Another shot rang from below. This one missed completely.

I glanced at Ethan's position on his ladder, slightly above me and to the left. He had his gun drawn. I craned my neck to try to see where he was pointing it at, but I couldn't spot anyone. He fired three bullets.

Someone made a cry of pain from below. Ethan must have scored a hit. He holstered his pistol.

"Nice shooting," I said, still trying to see where he had fired. A couple of buildings intersected into an alley, but the shadows concealed everything. "I couldn't see who was after me."

"That's why you have knights to defend you." Ethan grinned.

63

We descended the rest of the distance of the rope ladders without incident. The last rung hung a couple of feet off the ground. I hopped to the cobblestone street. Ethan and Marina flanked my sides. It felt good having them there.

"Lead the way," Marina said.

I nodded. We had to get to the palace, that's where my father would be in command. The palace would be closer to the center of the city, which wouldn't be too far at a brisk walk from where we'd been dropped off. I jogged down the street, and the others followed me.

We made quick time through the city until we crossed an intersection where I heard the *click* of several guns cocking. At that point, we slowed our paces.

"Stop and put your hands up!" someone shouted.

We complied and turned to see several members of the Grand Rislandian Army with their rifles pointed at us. "Hold your fire!" shouted their commander, keeping his palm open and up. He trudged toward us. "Captain Zaira von Monocle?"

I nodded to him and let my hands fall back to my side. "Sorry to scare you. We're trying to get to the palace to speak with my fa—the general."

The man nodded to me. He had a patch on his shoulder that signified his rank as corporal. "No problem, Captain von Monocle. The fastest route will be this way, behind where my men are set up. We have several troops staged on the rooftops to defend in case the Wyranth loop around and try to infiltrate the palace from the rear. We need to preserve our escape route to the north." His words hung in the air with the unsaid implication—*for when we lose the city.*

I couldn't think about that right now. I had to do what I could. "We'll carry on, then," I said.

He saluted me. "Good luck."

I returned the gesture, and we pressed onward toward the palace. Several more groups of soldiers spotted us along the way, some pointing and calling out for me, but they didn't stop us.

"It's strange seeing this place so ready for fighting," Marina said.

"Tell me about it," I said. "I'm just glad no one decided to shoot first before figuring out who we were."

Soldiers guarded the large, wooden palace doors and opened them for us. The long hallway was still marked by all of the flowery adornments it always had, tables with statues, paintings on the wall, something I'd not taken the time to stop and admire in full, even though I'd visited here frequently enough. Even with soldiers moving through, it felt empty without King Malaky and his servants buzzing about the long hallways.

We pushed past the door guards and into the war room. My father was there, along with Talyen, who was seated in a chair. Her hair was frazzled, and she had circles around her eyes, looking paler than usual, as if she'd been having trouble sleeping. I couldn't say I blamed her.

Her belly had swollen to such a point where I wouldn't be surprised if she had the baby right here. That was the last thing she or my father needed to worry about in the middle of this invasion. Dr. du Clockhand hovered over her with a cup of water, offering it to her. Talyen took it and drank. The High Knight stood off to the side of my father, along with several other high-ranking officers.

Marina and Ethan proceeded slowly, and they didn't look comfortable among all of the high-ranking soldiers. It didn't bother me any. I trudged right up to where my father planned alongside his other top military officials. Marina peeled off from Ethan, going to talk to Dr. du Clockhand.

"They've broken through the front gate but not the barricades as of yet," one of the soldiers said.

"To be expected," my father said. "It's good the airship arrived and slowed them down." He looked up and spotted me. "Ah, Zaira. Good timing."

"I'm here to help," I said.

"Not a moment too soon. You've seen the extent of the Wyranth force?" My father asked.

I nodded. It was unlike anything I'd ever seen before, and the worry in my father's eyes told me it was much the same for him, even with his years of experience.

"They're pulling out all the stops. I doubt we can defend the city." As if on cue, an ominous explosion sounded, rattling the walls. We all turned by instinct, but there was little we could do, and from here, we couldn't even see what was going on.

"I was hoping to find a bomb, like the one we used against the Wyranth in their territory when we rescued you. Remember?"

My father nodded. "I remember. But our weapons creation facility was sabotaged, just as you left."

I slumped my shoulders. "And that's where it would have been?"

One of the soldiers raised a hand. "Uh, sir?" he said. Everyone turned toward him. "There is a secondary storehouse. There might be a large bomb in storage and not in the production facility. Large explosives like this are expensive to make, though. The kingdom isn't in the habit of stocking them."

"It's worth a try," I said.

My father grinned. "Zaira, I swear, you think just like I do some days." He turned to the soldier. "Good suggestion, Corporal Tyson. You'll have to show us to the location of the storehouse." He paused at the sound of footsteps.

Another group of soldiers rushed into the room. Their uniforms were dirtied, wrinkled. They had rifles strapped to their backs. The first one came forward and saluted. "General von Monocle, sir."

"Go ahead, Private," my father said.

"The Wyranth have broken through the first barricade and are spreading into the city. There's too many of them. We're not going to be able to hold for long. Should we start the retreat plan?"

My father's eyes shifted to the model of Rislandia at a table beside him. It had markers that represented the troops of both nations. His fist clenched at his side. "We can't afford to lose," he said to himself.

The private cocked his head. "Pardon, sir?"

"Nothing," my father said. "Try to hold off a little longer. We might have a plan. Inform your superiors."

The private saluted. "Yes, sir." He spun on his heels and bounded out along with the others who had followed him in.

"I don't like being a general, Zaira," my father said. "Running an airship seemed so much easier. You could just fly off, have an adventure. Those were the good days."

I didn't know what to say. My father had never been ground-bound in my lifetime. It had to have been strange for him. But it was all strange for me, too. "So, this storehouse?" I prompted.

"Yes," my father said. "We'll go together. If we do find a bomb, you'll need help carrying the thing anyway."

"I was hoping to shoot up a flare and have the ship drop a rope," Ethan said.

"Smarter," my father said. "I was always a make-a-plan-and-figure-out-the-details-later kind of a captain."

"So's your daughter," Ethan said, mischievous eyes darting in my direction.

"Hey!" I said.

My father laughed. "Anyway. If everyone's ready..."

Talyen cleared her throat from where she sat. "I'm sorry, dear, but I'm not in much of a capacity to be running across streets in a war zone."

"Right," my father said. "Talyen, take two soldiers and commandeer a horseless carriage. Head for the retreat point and we'll meet you there. There's no sense in keeping you here if our lines are about to fail."

Talyen frowned. "I don't like this."

My father stepped to her, took her hands, bent down, and kissed the back of each of them before looking her in the eye. "I don't like this either. But we have to keep you safe."

Talyen made a face and gripped my father's sleeve. "I'd much rather be fighting. This is far more uncomfortable than having bullets shot in my direction."

"We're both fish out of water," my father said. "Or is it birds out of air?"

Talyen sighed. "Either way, we're not in our best elements. Help me up."

He assisted Talyen to her feet and into an awkward embrace. They kissed, a small peck. I didn't like watching it, but it was much better than having to see the locked lips of James and Princess Reina. *On my ship, at that!* Even though James and I had made peace, the image lingered in my mind and nauseated me. Some things I could never unsee.

Two soldiers came to Talyen's side, offering assistance, but she waved them off. She moved slowly, waddling back and forth from leg to leg. It was funny to watch her walk while pregnant, but we didn't have any more time to linger and be amused.

The High Knight had been quiet, observing us. He said his goodbyes and followed Talyen out the door. It was clear he would be protecting her, but it was left unsaid.

Our party became smaller, but Dr. du Clockhand and Marina stepped forward. "Pardon me, General von Monocle, sir," Dr. du Clockhand said. "I would like to take Commander Willet here and find Rhys. Under the circumstances, I think it would be safer for him and me to conclude our research aboard the airship at the conclusion of your mission."

"Very well," my father said.

"We'll look for the flare and meet you then," Marina said.

I nodded.

The two women took off toward another one of the large palace doors in the walls of this chamber.

I glanced to my father.

"Ready to save Rislandia, Zaira?"

I motioned toward the big double doors at the front of the room. "After you."

CHAPTER 12

Winter has slowed our army down. The Wyranth took advantage and there was a small skirmish south of Lakeside. I hope the rest of our army can travel soon.

An excerpt From Baron von Monocle's Log
Day 8 of the Month of Princesses
24th Year of King Malaky XV's Reign

WE HEADED BACK out into the streets. The soldiers had rifles, my father brandished his sword, and Ethan had a pistol in hand. I reached for my own pistol and gripped it tightly.

Shots fired repeatedly from somewhere, echoing through the empty streets. People were fighting and dying not too far from us.

Corporal Tyson led us to the secondary weapons storehouse, running with awkward, bird-like steps. He stopped himself at an intersection. From the right came a squad of Rislandian soldiers. They fired down the street to the left. When I caught up, I saw the Wyranth were advancing on our soldiers. They had a piece of artillery that chugged along on steam, a smokestack blowing exhaust into the air as its wheels turned down the street. A big rotary gun was mounted on it.

Two Wyranth soldiers fed bullets into the gun while another turned a crank. It blasted dozens of bullets at our army across the street. Some men were hit, others dove into broken shop windows or took cover under overhangs. They were helpless against the weapon.

Our saving grace was the Wyranth hadn't been expecting another group coming from our direction. We fired on all of them at the same time. The soldier turning the crank fell, and the rain of bullets stopped, allowing the Rislandians on the opposite side of the street to come out from cover. They started firing as well and, soon, the Wyranth were overtaken. A couple of the soldiers fled around a corner, avoiding our shots.

Corporal Tyson approached the other Rislandians. "Nice weapon they left here. Why don't we turn it around on them?"

The Rislandian nearest him grinned. "That sounds like a great idea." He motioned for his men to secure the piece of artillery. It had a bin full of bullets in the back that the Wyranth had been feeding into a tube behind it.

"Will they be able to operate it?" Ethan asked.

"Doesn't look too different from a standard horseless carriage. We saw how they turned the crank. Shouldn't be too hard," one of the soldiers said.

"Carry on, then," Corporal Tyson said. He waved us forward, and we continued toward the industrial district. So many windows were shattered, and the place looked so barren. The city looked very uninviting in this state, but it would be a prize for the Wyranth.

A blast sounded all too close to us, and one of Corporal Tyson's men fell. A second cried out in pain a moment later and dropped to the street.

"Snipers!" Ethan shouted. He pushed me under an awning. Several more bullets ricocheted off the street. My father and Corporal Tyson ducked into an alley nearby.

I saw movement up on the rooftops, but I couldn't get a good look. Ethan pushed me to the wall.

"Don't poke your head out," he said.

Part of me wanted to protest the way he'd pushed me aside, but he was right. Arguing in the middle of a fight didn't seem

like a good idea. I took a look at my surroundings. There was a
door behind us. I quieted my voice. "What if we went inside and
made our way up to the rooftop? We could take them by surprise,
especially if my father kept them busy down here."

"Great idea," he said.

"It is?" I looked at him hopefully.

"Yes, but I want you to stay here."

I narrowed my eyes at him. "Ethan..."

"I don't want you to take a risk at getting shot from up above,"
he said.

"I'm at risk getting shot down here, and besides, you're going
to take that risk."

"What's going on over there?" my father asked from his
concealment in the alley.

"Nothing!" I said. Another bullet whizzed by me as I spoke. I
backed into Ethan, falling into his arms.

Strong arms at that, holding me tightly even though he kept
his grip on his pistol. He looked down at me, his mouth agape. If
he was at a loss for words, so was I. His warmth gave me a great
sense of comfort, even in the middle of a battle. I could linger here
awhile if someone weren't trying to kill us.

"Let's go," I said, despite my urges to remain.

He released me and said no more about trying to keep me safe.
He motioned me aside and kicked in the door to the building.
Splinters flew and it swung away from us.

"Wow," I said.

"Things you learn to do as a knight." Ethan grinned. He moved
inside, and I followed him. It was a store with leather goods—caps,
goggles, satchels—and it all smelled very nice. But we weren't here
to shop.

Ethan weaved through the various tables of goods to the back
counter. Bat-wing doors concealed a back room. He moved right
for it. The doors swung after him, and I hurried to catch up.

Just as I'd hoped, we found a roof access ladder that went
straight to a hatch above. We climbed it quickly, the height being

nothing compared to what we were used to on an airship. The hatch wasn't locked, allowing Ethan to carefully pop it open a crack so he could look around.

"I don't see the shooter," Ethan whispered.

"He was shooting down at us at an angle. He's probably on the building across, yeah?" I said.

"Good point. We'll have to come out quickly. We don't want him picking us off as easy targets as we're trying to get our footing."

"I know how to enter into a fighting situation. I command an airship, remember?"

"Just checking."

He took a breath. "I'm going to rush up and fling the hatch all the way back on three. One... two..."

Ethan moved as fast as I'd seen anyone move before. His feet blurred as they darted up the final rungs of the ladder, and he came up onto the roof on his feet.

I muttered to myself that he had moved on the count of two as I tried to catch up with him. He fired two shots from the roof above.

"The shooter's on the building across from us!" Ethan said. A couple of shots fired back. Ethan dropped prone onto the roof just as my head popped through the opening. "Stay down," he said.

I crawled onto the roof rather than stood, seeing there was a raised ledge that provided us cover. Ethan crawled toward it, and I followed. When we were in position close to the edge, he glanced to the other rooftop. I took a moment to peek as well, seeing the roof with a wire dangling between the two, laundry dangling from it. On the other side was a small constructed enclosure that looked almost like an outhouse, though it wouldn't make sense to have one of those on a rooftop in the middle of the city.

Ethan fired a shot at the enclosure. Several birds flew out of it. "It's a birdhouse. Probably for carrier pigeons," Ethan said.

Which meant our shooter was hiding behind it. We needed to find a way to pry him out of there without getting shot. I found myself wishing for those explosive bags the Nightmen had, but

I hadn't even had time to report the existence of such weapons to my father, let alone present the idea to Rislandian scientists to develop them.

"What if I used that rope to go across and you kept him occupied back here?" I said quietly.

"That's crazy, Zaira. Too dangerous."

"I can do it. I've dangled on ropes like that before."

Ethan grimaced.

Why was I arguing with him anyway? My father wouldn't have argued with people when he had a plan. He would take action. I tried to sneak a glance over the side of the building. My father was still down there, looking toward the rooftop shooter and probably figuring out a plan of his own. But I was in the position to do something. I had to be decisive. "I'm going. Cover me," I said.

I scrambled for the clothing wire. It was secured by two bolts, one on each rooftop. It would hold from there, but was the wire strong enough for my weight? At least I had a lithe figure and was fairly short. James always used to lift me with no problem, back when we were on the farm.

Hand over hand, I moved forward. The wire sank some, but held. I wouldn't be able to keep upright, however. When I fully committed, I fell under the wire, dangling from it like one of the articles of clothing. My feet crossed around it behind me to help keep my balance.

Ethan fired a shot from behind me, keeping the shooter on the other roof at bay.

I tilted my head backward. Blood rushed to my head, but it was the only way I'd be able to see forward. Slowly, I moved one hand, and then another, carefully pushing clothing out of the way when I needed to. I couldn't dally, so I scooted across as quickly as I could.

My father caught a glimpse of me from down below. It looked like he mouthed, "That's my girl," to the people with him, but it could have been my imagination.

After several moments of crawling, I reached the edge. Sweat dripped down my forehead. The maneuver taxed me far worse than I'd thought it would. The gunman hadn't come out from behind his pigeon coop hiding place. Ethan kept me protected.

Now, how would I right myself to get onto this other rooftop? The angle I'd come in at made it tricky. I stretched my fingers out to try to get a grip on the rooftop, but there was little to hold onto. There was a protrusion made by the molding of one of the windows down below. If I could just get a foothold on it...

I clutched the wire tightly with both hands and let my legs drop. They dangled over the open air. Despite having been up higher in the air than most people ever would in their lifetimes, this height scared me. If I dropped, I would certainly break my legs or worse.

My body dangled in the air for far too long. The gunman came out and fired a shot, but he couldn't get at me before drawing Ethan's attention. Ethan returned fire. Bullets bounced off wood and brick. I couldn't see where they'd struck from my vantage but time wasn't on my side. If Ethan ran out of bullets, I'd be in real trouble.

I swung my legs back and forth, the wire moving with me. My foot almost caught the window ledge the first time, but when I swung again, I had far more momentum. I stuck both feet on the ledge. My shoes gripped onto the surface well enough to prevent me from swinging back, but it was difficult. Only one more maneuver and I'd have made it. I had to let go of the wire and get my hands onto the top of the roof.

Letting go proved to be the hardest thing I'd ever done. For the briefest moment, I could feel my body's weight shift. My stomach felt like it was going to drop right out of me, my head became dizzy. It could have been the end of me. My left foot couldn't keep on the molding, but I managed to cling to the corner of the roof with my fingertips. I dug in, my nails scraping and breaking from the strain. Pain jolted through my fingers, all the way up my arms.

JON DEL ARROZ

My fingertips would have slivers from this, but it was better than plummeting to my death.

I latched on with all my might and stabilized myself. Using my legs as leverage, I pushed upward and crawled onto the ledge.

The gunman poked his head out from behind the pigeon coop. He swung his arm out, the barrel of his gun pointed directly at me.

I rolled to the side, my legs dangling off the rooftop. He fired, and the shot bounced where I had been a moment prior. My heart raced. Too many close calls for too short a time. My von Monocle luck couldn't last forever.

As if the world sensed my thoughts, Ethan fired from behind me. His shot struck the gunman right in the hand. His pistol went flying. Now was my chance.

I pushed myself to my feet. The gunman cradled his hand under his arm, but with that other arm, he drew a knife. Ethan didn't fire another shot. I glanced behind to see a worried expression on his face as he kept his gun trained forward. Was he out of bullets? If he was, he had the sense not to say anything.

The gunman disappeared behind the pigeon coop. So he was going to make this a game.

I drew my pistol and jogged toward where he had been, giving the coop a wide berth in case he thought of popping out and surprising me. When I looped around the other side, I saw his pistol on the ground, and kicked it toward the opposite end of the roof. But the gunman still wasn't anywhere to be found. I stepped forward, out of Ethan's line of sight. Then the gunman jumped from the top of the coop.

He had a knife in his uninjured hand, and he dove straight for me.

Without thinking, I squeezed the trigger. It blasted him right in the shoulder. I stepped back and squeezed again.

The gunman staggered forward and dropped his knife. "You..." he said in between labored breaths. "You're too late. The kingdom's ours now. You'll never get it back."

He collapsed at my feet.

75

I holstered my pistol and sidestepped around him. We were safe now. As safe as could be with an invading Wyranth army blocks away from us. I tried to get a view of the city gates, but they were still too clouded with smoke and dust. The fighting must have been raging on, and perhaps my attacker was right. But I didn't have time to worry about it. We had to get down and find the bomb.

Surveying the roof, I spotted a similar hatch to the one we had climbed through about ten steps away from me. I'd be able to get back down without using the wire to swing across. I stepped to where Ethan could see me again and waved. "He's gone," I shouted.

"Good work. Need help getting back over?" Ethan yelled.

"No, I'm good. There's a hatch here."

"See you back on the street."

I nodded to myself more than to him. I crouched down beside the hatch and popped it open. This diversion had taken far too long. We needed to get to that bomb before the Rislandian forces were overwhelmed.

CHAPTER 13

Our scientists have developed an explosive with the capacity to cause a lot of damage. It's very unstable. My first officer isn't comfortable carrying it aboard the ship, but we must take risks if it means slowing the Wyranth.

An excerpt From Baron von Monocle's Log
Day 10 of the Month of Princesses
24th Year of King Malaky XV's Reign

ETHAN, MY FATHER, and the others waited for me when I returned to the street.

"Well handled, Zaira," my father said.

Ethan didn't say anything, but he didn't look nearly as happy with my heroics as my father did. I tried to ignore the look and continued down the street. Corporal Tyson took the lead again, and we hurried to the industrial district, where several large storehouses stood on each side of the street. No more snipers loomed on the rooftops along the way.

"That's the one," Corporal Tyson said, pointing to a building a few blocks down.

Metal clanked on the stone streets down the road. "Smoke bomb!" someone shouted from around a corner.

A metal canister spun on the ground in front of me. Smoke rose from it, filling the air. We were far enough back not to be impacted directly but silhouettes of men ran into the haze. Several gunshots followed. Were these friends or foes?

I looked to my father for guidance.

"Is there a back way to the warehouse?" he asked.

Corporal Tyson nodded. He led us down a side alley, winding us around to a dirt path behind a building. We were close to the city wall on the western side. When we came to the corner, Tyson stopped us with an outstretched arm. He pressed against the closest wall and peeked around the corner.

More gunshots came from the direction we'd just come from. The smoke from the projectile trickled higher in the air, creeping above the rooftops.

"Wyranth," Tyson said, turning back toward us.

"How many of them?" Ethan asked.

"At least eight. They're between us and the warehouse," Tyson said.

"Which means our army is on the other side, shooting in this direction through all that smoke," I said. We had to be careful, otherwise we might fall victim to a friendly bullet as easily as one from the Wyranth. But we also had an opportunity to help out our soldiers.

"We should take up positions and take down some of the Wyranth. Their flanked position will give us an advantage," my father said.

Corporal Tyson nodded. "Yes, sir." He readied his rifle.

Ethan moved to Corporal Tyson's side. One of the other soldiers handed him a freshly reloaded pistol. My father waited behind them, acting as a good general, but as I slid beside him, I could see in the corner of his eye that it pained him not to personally take a bigger stake in the action.

I dropped to a knee and drew my pistol, securing a spot between Ethan and Corporal Tyson.

"Fire on three," Ethan said, lowering his voice. "One. Two. Three."

Both of the men fired their guns. I took a second longer to pull my trigger. The Wyranth were lined up, not facing us, unmoving targets. They had taken their positions behind barricades they set up in the middle of the street, using the smoke as confusion, all of their fire focused toward the Rislandians facing away from us. Three of our shots struck different soldiers, who spun and fell in the street. The remaining Wyranth turned.

I scrambled back behind the building. Corporal Tyson spun to a safe position, and Ethan moved, as well. By the time return fire came, the Wyranth had no targets. Bullets whizzed by us.

"Good shooting," my father said. "Only now they know we're here!"

Our people fired more shots. A grunt of pain came from the Wyranth.

"They're advancing," one of the enemy soldiers shouted.

"Retreat!" another yelled.

"Get ready," Corporal Tyson said. He held his gun facing forward, narrowing his eyes.

Ethan and my father readied their weapons, and I did the same.

The Wyranth backed around the corner, still firing the opposite direction from us. They knew we were here, and a couple turned their guns quickly, but not before we could gun them down.

My heart pounded as a volley of gunshots came in our direction. One narrowly flew by my head, ricocheting off the wall behind me. The fleeing Wyranth soldiers collapsed to the ground in front of us, blood pooling around their bodies. One convulsed. Another still moved slowly, reaching for his gun he had dropped. I moved forward to try to keep the gun out of his reach, but Ethan grabbed me by the arm and held me back.

"You don't want to take friendly fire from our side," he said.

Corporal Tyson leveled his gun, pointing at the struggling Wyranth. His gunshot blasted. I turned my head so I wouldn't have to look. It was so brutal. I understood the precaution, but it felt wrong to watch an injured man go to his doom.

Heavy footsteps came forward from where the Wyranth had been.

"Rislandians?" Corporal Tyson asked loudly.

"Aye!" one shouted from behind.

"This is Corporal Tyson. Hold your fire. The enemy is down. We're behind the wall and coming out," Tyson said.

The Rislandians stopped moving from the other side. Tyson eased out, keeping his arms up, rifle in one hand, just in case they were jumpy. Ethan moved second, keeping himself squarely between me and the others. He wanted to protect me, which made me tingle with joy. Even though I could handle myself, it felt good to be cared for by someone so capable. I stepped forward along with my father.

We came face to face with nearly a dozen Rislandian soldiers. They had their guns pointed at us in precaution, but when they saw us, their unit commander raised a hand. "At ease," he told his men. They lowered their weapons. The commander stepped forward, saluting my father.

"At ease yourself, soldier," my father said, returning the salute.

"Sergeant Lansing, sir. Glad to see you, General von Monocle," the soldier said. "Those Wyranth held us off pretty well for being so few of them. They must have gotten through the main line. Caused quite a bit of trouble."

"How's the main line faring?" my father asked, his hand falling to his side.

Sergeant Lansing frowned. "Not well, I'm afraid. There's too many of them, even with our fortifications. It'll be a matter of time."

My father nodded. "We'll see if we can even the odds."

Sergeant Lansing raised a brow. "How can we help, sir?"

Corporal Tyson stepped forward. He motioned to a warehouse adjacent. "We can use your men to help lift a bomb out of here, if one remains in the storehouse. The *Liliana* is floating above the city. Our objective is to get a weapon aboard the airship."

"And then drop it right into the middle of the Wyranth forces," my father said.

Sergeant Lansing smiled. "I like this plan."

"Good, let's not delay," my father said. He motioned to Corporal Tyson. "Lead us in. For now, have your men fortify our position. Bring four in with us to help us move the bomb."

Lansing turned. "You heard them. Fan out and make sure this building stays secure. Singhal, Jennings, Babb, you're with me."

We followed Corporal Tyson into the storehouse's entrance. Inside, it was packed with different crates. There were hundreds of them, labeled with all sorts of supplies from military uniforms to grain.

"How are we going to find the bomb?" I asked.

"We'll all have to look. I know it's here somewhere. At least I hope it still is," Corporal Tyson said.

We spread out and began to look through all the supplies. Each of us took a separate aisle in the large storehouse. *Shouldn't it be easy to find a large bomb?*

"Over here," Sergeant Lansing said.

I cut through a small opening between several crates to cross into his aisle. Lansing stood with his hand atop a large metal cylinder strapped onto a pallet with several chains. It was as big as any one of us. "How heavy is it?" I asked.

The others arrived soon after I did.

Lansing rapped his knuckles on it. "Too heavy for us, I'd think."

Corporal Tyson was the last to arrive. Something whirred behind him.

I turned to see him pulling on what looked like a long cart, with two prongs protruding from the rear of it. The handle had several pipes and gears attached to it, which led down to a small steam motor on the side of it. It was power-assisted. "This lift will come in handy," Tyson said.

We gave him a wide berth so he could maneuver the lift toward the bomb. The wooden pallet was designed so the two protruding prongs could slip into it. Once they did, Tyson twisted the handle, which lifted the pallet off the ground. The engine clacked and whirred as it did so.

With the lift, he could carry the bomb entirely on his own. The rest of us walked with him.

"Suppose we didn't need a group of strong men after all," Lansing said.

"Never hurts to have back up," Tyson said.

Soon enough, we were back outside, flanked by the rest of Sergeant Lansing's unit. One of the soldiers whistled at the sight of the bomb.

"I bet that'll make quite a dent in the enemy forces," another soldier said.

"We'll see," Corporal Tyson said.

"Is there anything else supply-wise we might be able to use here?" I asked.

Tyson glanced around. "The warehouse is full of heavy munitions and parts for military vehicles. Cannonballs for your ship, but we might not have time to secure something so heavy along with the bomb."

I nodded. "Okay then."

Ethan stepped forward, pulling his flare gun from a clasp on this belt loop. "Everyone ready?" he asked.

Several nods and mutters of agreement followed.

He pulled the trigger and shot a flare into the air.

CHAPTER 14

News arrived that the knights were successful in destroying the Wyranth's artillery. We lost a lot of good men today. Tomorrow, we follow them by dropping our explosive into the Wyranth ranks. They'll never be prepared for this.

An excerpt From Baron von Monocle's Log
Day 12 of the Month of Princesses
24th Year of King Malaky XV's Reign

THE FLARE GLOWED in the low light of the early evening, a beautiful sight even through all the smoke. The beacon would lead the *Liliana* directly to our location. It had the potential to lead the Wyranth to us as well, but the airship wasn't too far off. I could already spot her silhouette to the north of us. They would arrive before anyone came to fight.

A hand clasped my shoulder. I turned to see my father.

"Zaira darling, I hate to leave your side, but I must prepare the rest of our troops here for evacuation," he said.

"Evacuation? But we have this bomb. We can stop the Wyranth."

"The troops we just met reported that a substantial number of Wyranth have already penetrated to the interior of the city. We may be too late for our defenses here. Even with the bomb, it may do little other than delay the inevitable."

I frowned, though I couldn't say I was surprised. I didn't want to admit to myself that our efforts could all be for naught. Even though slowing down the Wyranth forces would be invaluable, it seemed unfair to think we would lose Rislandia City no matter what we accomplished. My gut knotted as if someone had punched me. "Or it could give the troops the boost they need," I said.

"Our soldiers have seen how many forces they have out there, Zaira. I trust in their reports. They wouldn't give up if there were any way we could save Rislandia City. Don't worry, your actions will do good in the long run, but we need to regroup with the rest of our army if we're going to put a stop to their advance. My troops need me to lead them, Zaira."

"I... don't think I should retreat with you after this," I said, trying to think of the long-term plan.

My father watched me curiously. "Oh?"

"The Wyranth, they have more of that serum, right? It means there's another giant somewhere. I think the *Liliana* would be best suited to finding the giant and destroying it."

"Ah," my father said, smiling. "Proposing strategy. You've come a long way, Zaira." He held up a finger. "I should mention, my men interrogated the prisoner you brought to us. The Wyranth didn't know an exact location, but he seemed to indicate the vicinity of Plainsroad Village is the origin of the Wyranth's current supply of the serum. You might want to start there."

"Thanks," I said.

I didn't like the prospect of leaving my father in the middle of such an intense battle. Wouldn't it be better if he, as the general, traveled with us in the safety the skies provided? The Wyranth had no aerial vessel that could give chase. I opened my mouth to argue but closed it again. It wouldn't do for me to question his orders further. And knowing him, he would never leave his troops in the middle of a battle. He'd want in on the action himself.

Just like me, I realized.

I finally sympathized with how Lieutenant Colwell must have felt every time I insisted on going on a mission.

Maybe it was bad military etiquette, but I brought my father into a hug, wrapping my arms tightly around him. "I love you," I said, as if it were the last time we'd meet. I hoped that wouldn't be the case.

"I love you too, Zaira." He wrapped his bigger arms around me and gave me a squeeze before pulling back to give his men attention. "Alright, soldiers. Corporal Tyson, take half of Lansing's men and come with me. We're going to regroup with the main line. Lansing, guard my daughter and the bomb until they're both safely aboard the airship."

"Yes, sir," both of the men said. The soldiers split into two groups along similar lines as before. My father departed with Corporal Tyson and his team, heading deeper into the city. The smoke from earlier dissipated for the most part, but some haze still filled the air.

I let out a deep sigh.

"It'll be okay," Ethan said softly, stepping to my side.

Then there was a much louder *whir* than the one I'd heard from Corporal Tyson's lift. This one came from above. I looked up again to see the *Liliana* hovering over us. It amazed me how Major Ral was able to maneuver the ship with such precision.

Several ropes dropped from above. We had to secure the bomb to them.

"Will ropes be able to carry this thing?" I asked.

"Only one way to find out," Sergeant Lansing said. He went to work with one of his men, using the clips at the ends of our rope to attach to the chains around the bomb.

I heard the *clicks* of several of the soldiers readying their guns and spun around to see what made them jumpy. They had their guns trained down one of the streets, where three figures walked.

"Hold your fire," I said, though they were probably disciplined enough to not need my warning.

As the figures came closer, I saw Dr. du Clockhand, Marina, and Rhys, all with big bags slung over their shoulders, bursting at the seams with their scientific equipment.

I stepped forward past the line of men with guns. "Lower your weapons, these are friends," I said, stepping forward "Lieutenant Willet."

"Baronette," Marina said as she came closer. "I found them, and we also have some good news."

"At least there's something positive," I said. "What is it?"

Rhys beamed. "I believe over the last few days I've been able to produce a counter serum. It still needs further testing, but it's a step in the right direction."

"That is good news," I said. But when we get the opportunity to test the counter-serum? And how would we be able to make the Wyranth use it? Those questions would have to be answered when I had more time to think.

For now, I turned back around, seeing Sergeant Lansing had finished securing the bomb. The *Liliana* crew pulled it into the air. It swung back and forth. Dangerous. If it dropped while we stood here...

It wouldn't drop. These ropes were designed to lift weaponry like the bomb. We would be fine, but we had to go. Before I could step toward the rope ladder, the men had trained their guns in the direction the others had come from.

"Wyranth!" one of them shouted.

I glanced over my shoulder and saw a dozen or more enemy soldiers bounding down the street.

Our men wasted no time. They fired their rifles, hitting two of the lead Wyranth soldiers. The rest of the enemy contingent took up positions under awnings, around the building walls, and in the door frames. They had far better cover than we did.

"Hurry up and go," Lansing shouted.

I ran toward the rope ladders. We would be easy targets in the air if the Wyranth managed to get close enough. I had to trust in our soldiers, that they'd be able to keep us safe.

Rhys and the two women followed behind me. I was first to one of the rope ladders, with Ethan at my side. He gestured for the other three to take a second ladder. Marina led them to it, and we all started to climb.

Shots whizzed by us. I couldn't tell whether the Wyranth were aiming for us or for the Rislandian soldiers in the streets, and I didn't stop to take a look. I had to climb and move. There was nothing I could do to help the men below. I'd either make it up to the ship or I wouldn't.

I climbed as fast as I possibly could, but Ethan still managed to catch up with me. No matter how fast I went, I only slowed him down. He probably should have gone first.

A bullet grazed my ear.

At first, I thought I was done for. My knuckles went white, I gripped the rung of the ladder so tightly. The last thing I wanted to do was fall to my death. But I was still thinking, still conscious. The wound wouldn't kill me. But I'd stopped climbing, the worst thing I could do. I raised a hand to my ear. Hot blood seeped from the wound, but I couldn't see how bad it was.

"Zaira! Keep going!" Ethan shouted.

It hurt terribly, but it was just flesh. Nothing important. I clenched my teeth together hard, grinding them. The pain only seemed to get worse. My head throbbed. Tears filled my eyes, but I had to listen to Ethan. I couldn't afford to stay still.

Ignoring the pain as best I could, I climbed the ropes.

We soon rose far enough above the building tops to be out of range of the enemy rifles blow. It didn't stop the Wyranth from firing repeatedly, however. I couldn't look down and see whether we were winning the battle or not. I had to make it to the ship. My ear throbbed. By Malaky, how it hurt.

I looked to the side and saw that our other three companions were unharmed, still climbing, somewhat higher than us on the ladder. They hadn't stopped to nurse a wound. Before long, I reached the deck of the ship. A couple of deckhands grabbed my arms and hauled me aboard, and then assisted Ethan in the same way.

Ethan rushed to me, tilting his head to get a glance at me. He brushed my hair back over my ear. His eyes dimmed into serious concern.

"Did they blast it clear off?" I asked.

"Just a lot of blood. Most of your ear is still there. I think the top might look a little strange once it heals," he said.

At least he was honest.

My ear throbbed, but I did my best to ignore it. I turned back around, sidestepping toward some of the railing to peer over the side. Only a few of our men seemed to remain, and they were on the run through the streets of Rislandia. The Wyranth force gave chase, overwhelming the poor Rislandians. We wouldn't have lasted much longer if we'd remained down there.

The crew pulled the rope ladders up, which didn't allow any Wyranth to get to them. The bomb swayed just below the bottom of our hull. It was dangerous, even there. If the Wyranth had any weaponry that could reach this far, our whole ship would blow.

"Ethan, tend to Marina and the others and get them situated. I have to get to the bridge."

He didn't argue with me, nodding, and heading for our friends. I bounded the opposite direction and made my way inside the small bridge compartment.

"Glad you made it back safely," Lieutenant Colwell said once he saw me, then narrowed his eyes. "What happened to your ear?"

"Shot," I said. His words reminded me of the pain I tried so hard to ignore.

"I swear, you take more bullet wounds than our commandos. It's like they're drawn to you," he said, shaking his head. "You know—"

I waved him off. "Yes, yes. As the airship captain, I should stay aboard and not risk myself. You'd be horrified with what I did down below. I'll tell you later. For now, we need to get moving."

"Is Dr. du Clockhand back with you? If so, you should see her and make sure it doesn't get infected," Lieutenant Colwell said in a chastising tone.

"When I have time," I said sternly.

He grimaced, as if realizing it wouldn't do any good to lecture me. "I see we were able to procure a bomb."

I nodded. "We were. Which means we need to fly right over the Wyranth and drop it on them."

"We're not going to be able to load it into one of our cannons. We're not equipped right now for—"

"Not a problem," I said. "These things detonate on impact, right? We just need to get up high enough and cut the ropes."

"We can't be as accurate that way."

"We don't really have a choice," I said, turning to the major. "Major Ral. Take us up, preferably out of range of anything the Wyranth can throw at us, and hover above their army outside the front gates."

"Aye, Baronette," Major Ral said. He moved the levers, and the airship lifted further into the air.

The crew scurried outside the window, aware we were about to go back into the battle zone. They reminded me of my ferret in some ways, and I was glad the little critter was in my room. At least I hoped he was. He had a habit of escaping during battle, not that I expected any action on the bridge of the ship.

We lifted into the clouds. The forward motion kicked in, pushing us through the puffy white masses. Down below, Wyranth flooded the gates of the city like little ants. The stream had broken through into the southern section of the city, where tiny flashes of light burst—gunfire between the two armies. The Grand Rislandian Army looked overwhelmed from this distance.

Lieutenant Colwell peered through the telescope. "This is about as good as we're going to get without risking too much damage to the city itself," he said.

Major Ral pulled back on the lever. The ship stopped its forward movement and hovered in the air.

"Order the bomb's ropes cut," I said.

Colwell nodded and jogged out of the bridge. He raised his voice to compensate for the turbine noise, shouting his orders. The deckhands moved to the side rails. A couple of them produced knives, cutting into the rope that held the bomb. The rope became thinner and, eventually, one side snapped.

I moved to the side window. The bomb swung over the side. It was dangerous because if it hit our hull with too much pressure, it could explode and bring us down. They really should have tried to make both ropes cut simultaneously, but it was too late for that. I winced, watching the bomb scrape against the hull when it rocked backward.

Then the second rope gave way.

The bomb dropped through the air, becoming smaller in my field of vision.

"It's away," I said.

Major Ral put the ship back into gear, restoring our forward motion. We didn't want to be directly over the blast, just in case.

"Turn the ship so I can see," I said.

He did, and I saw a plume of smoke rising from the ground below. It'd landed directly in the heart of the Wyranth forces. Just like before, the people scattered everywhere. We had to have done a significant amount of damage. I didn't even want to think about the amount of lives we had to have taken.

Lieutenant Colwell returned to the bridge, and then moved back to the telescope. "Direct hit," he said. "You placed the ship very well, Major Ral."

"Thank you," Major Ral said.

He turned the telescope so he could get different views.

"Well?" I asked. "What's going on?"

"The Wyranth aren't backing down. There's a large hole in their ranks at the wall, but there's a significant portion of them already through. The city's overwhelmed."

I wrinkled my nose. "I wish we had one more bomb."

"I wish I had a horseless carriage and a pile of gold to fill the back trunk, which I'd take to my beach house in the Tyndree Kingdom," Lieutenant Colwell said, "but it wouldn't do any good. We couldn't drop a bomb within the city or what would be the point?"

"You have a beach house?" Major Ral asked.

"It's an expression."

"Oh. Sounds nice," Major Ral said, frowning.

I didn't see how the men could joke at a time like this. Our efforts hadn't been enough. Rislandia City would fall to these crazed soldiers. Just like my father had said. And all we could do was sit here and watch from up in the sky. It wasn't fair. It wasn't right. And worse, my ear hurt. I wanted to cry.

The bridge fell to silence for several long moments. It seemed like my men finally realized how grave of a situation we were in. We were giving up on Rislandia City, a place we had once thought to be impenetrable. But I had my plan, and the blessing of my father to carry it out. The *Liliana* would make a difference if it were the last thing we did. "We have Rhys and Dr. du Clockhand back aboard. They can help us take away some of the Wyranth's advantage," I said.

"Are you speaking of their soldier serum?" Lieutenant Colwell asked.

I nodded. "Exactly. Rhys said they were close to finding a cure for the addictions. If we can cut off the Wyranth supply and develop one, that would do more to turn the tide of the battle than regrouping up north."

"Sounds easier said than done," Lieutenant Colwell said. "And I might advise you that as the kingdom's sole airship, we should probably get orders from General von Monocle."

"I already ran it by him," I said, looking him in the eye.

"I know that look."

I ignored him and paced the small area of the bridge. "We're heading south. It'll be a scouting mission at first. We have to see if we can spot some supply caravans. If they do have a new supply of this serum, it has to be coming from somewhere. Which means we can pinpoint it from the sky. It'll take hard work, but our people can do it," I said.

Lieutenant Colwell nodded. "It's not a bad plan."

"Good. Have the commandos on a watch rotation on the deck so we can have more eyes on the road below," I said. "Major Ral?" I turned to the pilot. "Set a course for us toward Plainsroad Village. Bring us up into the clouds so we aren't an easy target for Wyranth artillery that might spot us. We'll loop around that countryside until we spot their supply chains. If you need me, I'll be with Dr. du Clockhand getting my wound dressed."

CHAPTER 15

The explosive proved too volatile. While it didn't detonate aboard the ship, it did before it reached ground. The Wyranth panicked from the explosion in the sky all the same and retreated back to Desert's Watch. For now, we have a brief respite from battle.

An excerpt From Baron von Monocle's Log
Day 13 of the Month of Princesses
24th Year of King Malaky XV's Reign

AFTER LEAVING DR. du Clockhand, I opened the ship's log book and wrote down all I could recall about the Battle of Rislandia City. *Was that how battles were named?* Someone just wrote what they thought it should be called and it ended up in history books? It felt strange to think that my logs might one day be in someone's academic writings somewhere.

Writing wasn't very fun for me, all the same. When I first started making the logs, I flipped through the book to see how my father did it rather than come up with my own style of writing. His logs were so to the point, creating a great narrative. I didn't know how to describe the battles nearly as well as he could. Moreover, my hand started to cramp from clutching the pen every time I wrote. I resigned myself to fairly brief logs, and then set my pen down. With at least a couple more hours before the *Liliana* would reach the area surrounding Plainsroad Village, I had little to do. So I flopped down on my bed.

Within moments, Toby skittered out from his hiding place beneath the bed and leapt onto my stomach. His claws dug into my blouse, pricking my skin, but not hard enough to draw blood. I yelped in surprise, despite expecting the move. Toby always tried to get as close to me as possible. And these last few days, I hadn't had much time to pay attention to him.

I squeezed the little critter so tightly he tried to wiggle out of my grasp. I laughed, releasing him. "Oh, Toby. How did we get into this mess?" I said.

He chirped in response, crawling up my chest, sniffing at my chin. His wet nose tickled me.

I snuggled with him, not squeezing him as hard as before, and he curled into a ball on me. A warm ball at that. His warmth made my eyes grow heavy and, soon, I found myself snoozing.

It was a shift in the airship's momentum that woke me. I jolted awake. How long had I been out?

I glanced to the portal at the back of my cabin. It was dark out, the moon shining over the Rislandian landscape. I'd caught a couple of hours sleep at least. We must have arrived at Plainsroad Village.

Toby was still asleep on me, but I tilted my body, causing him to fall onto my bed. He squawked in protest.

"Sorry, Toby," I said, standing. "I have to get to the bridge."

Not looking back at him—because his little cries for me would likely break my heart—I trudged toward the door. Once outside, I carefully shut it behind me. The tight hallway was devoid of any crew, empty. After our hard battle, most would be eating in the mess up top or would be out on the deck to get the view of the stars.

I jogged through the halls and up the stairs until I reached the deck and found my crew out there as I'd expected. Several of them saluted as I made my way to the starboard guardrail to get a look over the side.

The countryside was dark under the moonlight, but still shined with the hint of green brought on by the winter rains. It seemed so empty, though. The buildings I'd grown up with were no longer there, not since the Wyranth ran their war machines through the tiny village.

There used to be a schoolhouse just beyond the creek. We had a market square, a town hall, and an inn—all gone now. The road that bisected the buildings remained. Despite not having come here in months, it tugged on my heart to think of Plainsroad Village being erased from existence. I had so many memories here.

And what happened to the people? I'd known my neighbors, the Gentrys, were overwhelmed by Wyranth, but did others escape? I wanted to see my former teacher, Miss Penniesworth, most of all.

"Let's land," I told my crew.

Sergeant Wright stood close by. He motioned one of his privates over to him. "Go tell Major Ral the Baronette orders the ship be set down," he said.

"Aye, sir," said the private with a salute. He hurried toward the bridge.

I couldn't keep my eyes off the scene below. Why had the Wyranth razed the place to the ground? It didn't have any tactical purpose. It's not like any of the soldiers remained here.

But I knew the answer. Their serum made them crazed, more violent than they would be otherwise. Nothing mattered for them except for bloodshed, the thrill of fighting.

I'd had a little of the serum once. The *Liliana's* medic gave it to me to help heal my wounds. It had put overwhelming pressure on my mind just having it one time. The way it clouded my mind and made me want to lash out was awful. It took all control away from me. I could only imagine what a regular dose would do to a person.

Ethan von Lantern stepped to my side. He stretched a hand toward me, as if he wanted to touch or console me, but he stopped himself. It wouldn't be appropriate with so much of the crew on the deck, and I was glad he understood that. "Are you alright?" he asked.

"It's hard seeing the place I grew up like this. Everything's gone," I said.

"I understand," Ethan said, but a wavering in his voice told me he didn't.

How could he? If he hadn't seen this himself for his own hometown. But he must worry that something similar had happened to his. All of Rislandia was in danger of becoming like Plainsroad Village.

The airship descended, dropping onto some flat fields. At first, I wanted to protest to protect the crops, protective as I would be if I still had a farm life here. But then, whose crops were they? These overgrown fields served no one now. Or worse, they may have supplied the Wyranth. As we came closer to the ground, more of the crew came to look over the side rails. I peered out onto the horizon. I hardly recognized this place as home and it had only been a few months.

One building still stood, however, not too far from where we landed. A small silhouette in the evening. I recognized it even without much light. My eyes went wide. "My house," I said.

"Huh?" Ethan asked.

"That's my house over there," I said, pointing toward the building. "I can't believe it's still there. I want to go see it." Those words sounded foolish to me, as I understood we had a mission to accomplish, and I shouldn't be taking time from that for some fancy of seeing my old life. When I turned to Ethan, however, I saw no judgment in his eyes.

"I'll come with you," he said.

"Really?"

He nodded. "It'll be interesting to see the home of the great Baron von Monocle."

I smiled. "It's not as interesting as it sounds." But if he wanted to come with me, I wouldn't turn him away. I liked having Ethan by my side, supporting me. It made me feel safe, even in the face of this Wyranth invasion.

The *Liliana* landed, shaking as it touched down, but not jolting me very much.

"It really is amazing how precisely he can make these landings," Wright said to one of his commandos.

I turned to Wright. "Gather a scouting party and see if you can find any evidence of Wyranth. I'm going to, uh…" I tried to think of an excuse.

"Visit your home, no doubt," Wright said with an understanding nod. "The night is a perfect time for reconnaissance as it is. We'll check back in a few hours and report our findings."

I nodded. "Excellent." The crew moved away from the rails, some to attend to their duties, others heading toward the mess. I headed for the stairs and off the ship toward my old life.

CHAPTER 16

I returned to Rislandia City to see my dearest Liliana for the Winter Festival. She hates the city, and come summertime, she wishes to move to the countryside. King Malaky promises that if we can overcome the Wyranth, he will reward me with lands. I may be able to give Liliana what she wants after all.

An excerpt From Baron von Monocle's Log
Day 17 of the Month of Princesses
24th Year of King Malaky XV's Reign

SINCE NO ONE spotted any Wyranth in the immediate area, I decided to bring Toby with us. The poor little critter had been cooped up far too long with all the fighting going on. He was happy enough to run around, sniffing his way through the fields. Sometimes he followed dutifully, but more often than not, he needed a stern reminder to keep up with us.

It wasn't long before we approached my old home. Seeing the place gave me the chills like I had seen a ghost. I held my lamp up to cast more light on the house in the darkness.

It was a tiny place, much smaller than the apartment building where I resided in Rislandia City. The house only had three rooms, as we hadn't needed more than the basic necessities for survival. My neighbor, Mister Gentry, had stored all of my crops for sale in the market in his barn, which meant we never had to build one of our own, either. All things considered, my life hadn't been terrible, even growing up without parents.

The paint was starting to fade, which it probably had been before I'd left, but I'd never noticed. The roof still had the hole in it from earthquake damage. In the time since I'd been there, someone had broken one of the windows. The front door was slightly ajar. I pushed it open.

The air was stale inside, dusty. No one had been in here for a long time, but what I saw shocked me.

My table was overturned, picture frames lay shattered and fallen to the floor. Chairs were ripped apart. Cupboard doors and drawers were left open, with all of the contents spread over the counters.

Someone had ransacked the place.

"You're not very organized, are you?" Ethan asked from behind me.

The sight shook me. Looters couldn't even leave my home alone? It was in such disrepair I found the sight to be painful. My chest hurt.

"Very funny," I said, stepping into the mess, careful to veer away from the shards of glass all over the floor. I stopped and bent down to pick up one of the pictures. Turning it toward me, I saw the face of my mother staring back at me. I couldn't help but have a little lump form in my throat.

"She's pretty," Ethan said.

"Yeah."

"You look a lot like her. Same chin and eyes."

I looked back to Ethan. Did he just say I was pretty? It sounded like it. His brown eyes were very intent on me. Serious, concerned. Loving? Whatever his expression, it made it very hard for me to remember to breathe.

He brushed the back of his fingers against my cheek. My heart beat faster than the *Liliana's* turbine gears turned. What was happening?

Before I could say anything, or even figure out what to do, Ethan bent close to me. His lips touched mine. The tingling in my face was like a thousand fireworks went off inside me all at once. Was he kissing me? I almost forgot to respond, but I returned the kiss, rocking to the tips of my toes, bringing me closer to him. The moment wasn't long, but it made all the blood rush to my head.

He pulled back and looked at me intently again. "You have no idea how long I've wanted to do that."

I had no idea how long *I'd* wanted him to do that. My heart was still pounding, reverberating in my chest. I became self-conscious, like he could hear it, and stepped away from him, turning back to the cluttered mess of my home. I didn't know what to say, so I changed the subject. "Someone went through here. I'd venture to guess it was the Wyranth when they were coming after me. Maybe they were looking for information on the airship. They must have thought there were some great state secrets in here or something."

Ethan stepped through the house. His lips were tight together, but he didn't say anything. Had I offended him by not being more direct? I had no idea how to handle boys. All James and I ever did was tease each other, but that didn't seem appropriate here. If he was upset with me, he didn't say anything. "I would do the same if I were them. Was there anything of value?"

I shook my head. "Not to my knowledge. My father rarely came home, and he'd been in prison for two years before this happened. It's just so odd to see it like this."

"I'm sure," Ethan said.

I took a deep breath. This house was the past. I had to let it go as surely as I'd had to let my mother go when she'd died, or when I'd thought my father was gone, as well. My home was aboard the *Liliana,* with Lieutenant Colwell, Major Ral, Harkerpal, First Sergeant Wright, and... Ethan. Was he a permanent fixture in my world now? I brought my fingers to my lips.

Ethan paced around the area, finding his way to a shelf where a few books still stood. He picked up one of them. "A history of the Rislandia-Wyranth peninsula. Huh. We're supposed to be acquainted with this as knights, but because of the war efforts, I've been pressed into service and had to skip a few of the standard classes."

"You can bring it with you if you like. I'm not sure how much time you'll have for reading, though."

"True," he said, tucking the book under his arm. "Thanks."

I motioned to the door. "We should get going. There's nothing to help our mission here."

"At least you have some closure, and know the place is still standing. Maybe when the war's settled…"

I shook my head. "When that happens, we'll go exploring."

"We?" The corner of Ethan's mouth ticked upward into a half-smirk.

Concentrating proved impossible. I couldn't look at anything. Ethan had *kissed* me. What did this all mean? My head swam with emotion. My face felt as if it would soon burn off of me. We still had my parents' former room and my own room to search, but…

"Wait a second," Ethan said. He peered into my parents' room. "There's a little compartment under the floor, under the rug. There's a little crease that gives it away. Do you see it? It's very difficult to spot."

I watched him. He moved into the room. After getting to his knees, he rolled back the rug popped open the floor. Sure enough, there was a little compartment. Inside was a small, leather-bound book and a mask.

I followed over to him, holding my lamp up, still lost in my thoughts—or lack of thoughts, as it may be.

The mask was obviously something designed for a woman. Porcelain white, with a floral painted pattern on it. I couldn't help but take it from him. Ethan let go easily, more interested in the book. Was this my mother's? It was dusty but so beautiful. I decided I would take it with me and ask my father what it had been for when I saw him next.

Ethan thumbed through the pages. "This looks like schematics. For airships."

"You'll probably want to take that, too. It could come in handy later," I said.

"I'm sure your father would appreciate having it," Ethan said, taking the book and standing. "We should do one more thorough search, just to make sure we didn't miss anything."

Ethan cocked his head at me. "Are you okay?"

"Yeah. It's hard seeing my home like this, is all." It was true, but I needed a little bit of space from him to think as well.

"I get it," Ethan said. He frowned but set to searching the main room again.

I wiped a tear from my eye as I went back outside. For years I'd lived here, worked here. I hated seeing my home in tatters, even if I didn't feel this place was where I belonged any longer.

I turned my eyes to my fields, now overgrown with grasses. The moonlight shone down on them. Without thinking, I walked toward those fields where I used to grow my crops. I'd had a heavy tomato harvest, some of the best in the region, and Mr. Gentry helped me sell them at the Plainsroad Village market. I missed him and Mrs. Gentry too.

"Lovely night, isn't it?" a voice said from behind me.

A chill ran up my spine. That voice… I spun.

Ivan, the Iron Emperor of the Wyranth Empire, stood before me. He was alone, and he walked toward me with the confidence of a hunter descending on prey.

My hands shook, but I pulled my pistol from its holster and pointed it directly at him. "What do you want?" I asked.

"Now, now," Ivan said. "If you think I came here alone, you are sorely mistaken. You can strike me down, but my snipers will take care of your friend inside the moment something happens to me. We wouldn't want that, now would we? Don't think about yelling for him either. You won't like the results."

I bit my lip. How dare he? After all he'd done to me. All the pain he'd caused, and worse, the fact that he'd set me on a mission away from my people. For a brief moment, I thought about shooting him anyway.

Not at the cost of Ethan, though. I lowered my pistol.

"Very good," Ivan said, his voice quiet. "Now what's this I hear about a book?"

"None of your business. I'm not going to fall for any of your schemes again."

He chuckled as he stepped very close to me. He put both of his hands on my arms.

I tensed.

"Zaira, I did not become emperor merely because of succession. I fought for what I wanted, and I will still fight for what I want. What I want is peace. Is that so much to ask?"

"Liar," I breathed.

He looked me in the eye with those deep pools, the most beautiful eyes I'd ever come across. Why did they have to be on such a wicked man? It made me all the more sick to be forced to gaze into them. "We have plans here in the north, and they're coming to fruition. I know you must be terribly angry with me, but your trip to Zenwey was, at the time, mutually beneficial for both of us. You shouldn't be hard on yourself. I've heard your exploits there were rather remarkable."

"What do you want?"

He dropped his arms to his sides. "I told you, peace. It's not too late, Ms. von Monocle. You can still attain it through marriage to me."

"Are you still on that? Aren't there plenty of women in your empire to choose from?"

Ivan paced around me. His eyes fixed on me as if surveying cattle at market. I held still. "None with fire in their souls. None with such tenacity. None with the heritage of the von Monocle. Don't you wish to rule not only one, but two kingdoms?"

"I have no interest in such things." I held my chin high.

"Which makes you all the more attractive, I assure you. You're approaching your last chance, however. I grow tired of games, and I grow even more tired of the pitiful defenses Rislandians put up.

The plan I have in motion will be this land's downfall. I don't want this to happen."

"Then leave us alone."

"I'm afraid that's impossible. I don't know if you've seen my empire, but much of it is uninhabitable. With our newfound industry, we've also had our population swell. We need breathing room."

I didn't say anything. Was this all a land grab? These generations of war?

"I know what you're thinking, but I'm thinking about the long-term well-being of my people. It's far more important to me than some petty morality. Regardless, there is still time. I have messengers everywhere. If you change your mind, send a post. I will be waiting for you. At some point, I will find your weakness, and I will seize your heart." He clenched his fist in the air.

He was absolutely insane.

I held still as he walked away, not sure what else I could say. He knew about the book Ethan found. What else did he know? I wished I'd been able to grill him about what he did, why he put me in this position where I'd kept our meeting a secret. I felt like a traitor. But what could I do? It didn't look like there were any snipers around, but I didn't want to take the risk.

He disappeared into my fields.

Ethan stepped out of the house a moment later. "Zaira?" he asked. "You look like you've seen a ghost.

"I think I have," I said, swallowing a lump in my throat. "Let's get out of here."

"Don't you want to see your old room? You didn't even go inside."

I shook my head. "There's nothing for me here anymore. I need to move on with my life." And stop this plan the Iron Emperor had before it was too late.

"Suit yourself," he said, though he sounded concerned. Ethan didn't argue, however, but clutched the books between his arm and body and trudged back toward the *Liliana*.

Along the walk back to the *Liliana*, I didn't once stop to look back. Though the main village had been leveled, several of the houses on the outskirts remained intact. Even with several houses around, the soul of the town had been destroyed. *Just like Portsgate. And how many other towns?* However many it was, we couldn't let it happen to any more. The Iron Emperor had to be stopped.

Ethan and I didn't talk much on the walk back, either. I don't know if it was the kiss making matters awkward, or if we were both too caught up in our worries, but there was little to say. I still found myself to be in shock from Ivan's appearance. He wanted me to be second guessing myself, though. This was all a ploy to get in my head, just like last time. I didn't want to think about him anymore. I wanted to think about Ethan.

It struck me that outside of a few tidbits of information, I didn't know much about Ethan. He talked about his knight training fairly often, and with fondness, and he came from a noble line in order to have a surname like von Lantern bestowed upon him by King Malaky. But who was he before? What were his hopes for life outside of this war? Were there any? I found myself side-glancing at him.

"What are you thinking about?" Ethan asked.

"Just how little I've really gotten to know... anyone aboard my ship," I said. It was a half-truth, but he didn't need to know he was on my mind. "I know Lieutenant Colwell has a family, and that Harkerpal has dedicated himself to the airship more than anyone else alive, but we used to have lives outside of this whole mess, didn't we?"

Ethan laughed. "I guess we did. Mine was just playing in the yard until my father sent me off to a boarding school in Rislandia City. Cid stopped by the school one day, spotted my athletic abilities, and tested me for entry into the knights."

"Yeah, I guess most of my life was work until recent times, too. I mean, if you count school as work. I do."

"I do too. I don't much like being cooped up inside a classroom."

"I never did either," I said.

"I could see that. You're always trying to get into the action, not afraid to get your hands dirty. I like that about you."

I felt my cheeks growing hot from the compliment. "Thanks."

"And we're not all expecting you to listen to our life stories, you know. You're captaining an airship. That takes a lot of time and energy. You're not neglecting anyone."

Was that what I feared? I'd been worried about my personal relationships even since our big expedition over to the Zenwey continent. I'd had less time to focus on people since then. My friendship with James Gentry had certainly become a casualty of my time. But maybe he was just a type of person who was needier than Ethan. It made sense. He'd lost his parents, had no one to cling to. It made me feel slightly guilty to be thinking about him around Ethan, but I hadn't done anything wrong, had I?

The last thing I could afford were feelings in the middle of this war. Why was this happening to me now of all times?

Before we could chat further about our personal lives, we came to the airship. It had lights on, beacons for us to find the *Liliana* in the moonlight. I picked up the pace, starting to run.

"Hey," Ethan said. "What's your hurry?"

"I just want to get back to the ship," I said. He took it as a challenge, as if it were a race and something to laugh about. For me, running meant exerting myself. I tried to shed the pain of the Iron Emperor's visit. Most of all, I wanted to be back in the safety of my airship with my crew.

CHAPTER 17

Finally, the army has arrived in the south. The southern area around Lake Bethany is now fortified. We're as prepared as we can be.

An excerpt From Baron von Monocle's Log
Day 25 of the Month of Princesses
24th Year of King Malaky XV's Reign

FIRST SERGEANT WRIGHT and his team were already at the ramp when we arrived. It would still be a few hours before sunrise, and we all were tired. But most of us were still too on edge to sleep. The crew had started a nice bonfire just by the ship, and a lot of them were gathered around, eating, drinking, and enjoying these brief moments of respite. There was a sense that these could be our last, and we should share them together.

Rhys and Marina stood by the fire. Rhys had his arms around her waist, whispering something into her ear. Marina giggled. At least they'd found happiness through all this. I resisted the urge to sneak a glance at Ethan.

I approached the fire, and the crew greeted me warmly. I wasn't much in the mood for socializing, but I didn't want to let on to the crew that there was something wrong. How could I explain to them that I'd had the Iron Emperor in my sights and I let him go? Again.

107

Harkerpal gave me an enthusiastic wave before sipping from his steaming mug. His junior engineers gathered around him, and he soon fell into what no doubt was a long tale about the *Liliana's* past exploits under my father. It was something I didn't need to listen to at the moment.

Instead, I veered toward First Sergeant Wright, who had a map sprawled out over the ground. Two of his commandos huddled near him. They looked like they were making plans.

When Wright saw me, he saluted me. "Baronette," he said.

"You found something, I take it?" I asked.

He nodded. "Yes, my people spotted a caravan of Wyranth just to the east of here. I don't think they saw us. I sent two of my best scouts to tail them. As soon as the Wyranth reach their destination, the scouts will report back. They know what to look for. A factory of some sort distilling the soldier serum. All we have to do now is wait."

"Great," I said and helped myself to a seat in the grass by the fire. It burned hot, the wind blowing its flames and the smoke away from me. It felt good to be by the warmth.

As we waited, crew came and went. The chef prepared meals outside, allowing us all to eat, and for those interested in consuming alcoholic beverages, to have them. Several people drifted off to bed during that time, some of the crew taking turns keeping watch. I couldn't sleep, and I did my best to keep myself clear-headed, as did most of the commandos. We had to be ready to go on a moment's notice. They likely wouldn't assume I'd go with them, but I would spring it on them when the time came.

The sun crept over the horizon, bathing the area in morning light. Our airship still cast a shadow over where we stood. Dr. du Clockhand appeared from the bowels of the airship, coming and taking a seat next to me.

"We're close to finding another one of those giants you keep mentioning?"

"I hope so," I said.

"Me as well. Working with Rhys has been incredible. He has a talent with chemistry. Under normal circumstances, I believe we could make great advances in medicine together. But if we can cure the Wyranth of this madness that consumes their armies, it will make a difference enough for now," Dr. du Clockhand said.

"That it will. We could all use some good news right now, at the very least."

"I agree. I wonder what happened to the prisoners and patients at my hospital," she said, frowning. The way the flames of the bonfire moved cast shadows across her face.

"What do you mean?"

"They weren't evacuated with everyone else. No one knew what to do with them. Part of the cost of war. No one thinks about the infirm or those without homes." Her eyes looked like they were about to water.

"I'm sorry," I said, and I was. It hadn't occurred to me to think of those displaced by the war, who had their lives upended. We had rescued a little girl back in Portsgate who'd lost her family. What had happened to her when we dropped her off in Rislandia City? My shoulders tightened and my stomach hurt when I thought of her. I hadn't checked in on her. There'd been no time. But how awful was it that I couldn't find time for a little girl with no family, no hope?

"No, I'm sorry," Dr. du Clockhand said, tilting her head to look at me. "I can see I've upset you. You don't need more weight on your shoulders."

I stared at the fire for some time before responding. "No, it reminds me what I'm fighting for. Just how much every life matters. We can't leave them to the Wyranth."

"And we won't," Dr. Du Clockhand said. "Everyone has tremendous faith in you. They know you'll find a way."

A lump grew in my throat. I was everyone's hope? I'd barely accomplished anything in my time in command of the *Liliana*. "I'll do my best," I said.

Rustling in the fields beyond distracted several of the crew, who pointed in that direction, away from the fire and into the darkness. I pushed myself to my feet and dusted the dirt off of my pants and cape.

"What is it?" Dr. du Clockhand asked.

I offered my hand to her to help her up, and she took it. She wasn't all that heavy, and lifting her to her feet proved easy. "I think it's our returned commandos," I said. Wright said he'd sent some scouts into the forest.

She backed up to allow me space. I turned and stood on the tips of my toes to try to look over the shoulders of some of the others standing between me and the commotion. Sure enough, our commandos walked toward us. They greeted First Sergeant Wright and some of the others.

I maneuvered my way through the crew to meet them, and they saluted us. A muscular commando stood to face the front of the group.

"Corporal Perry," Wright said, addressing the muscular man. "Report."

"We came across a Wyranth vehicle—steam powered—and followed it off the main road for several miles down to an iron mine set between two hills. There were several Wyranth stationed there, perhaps twenty in total. I don't believe most of them were soldiers. They have four standing guard, but the others looked more like general laborers. The vehicle's occupants conducted some business and left. From our further scouting, we did see barrels, which contained large amounts of the blue serum you told us to look out for."

"That's it," I said.

"It's a good lead," Wright agreed. "And a small force. It would be something our airship could handle, no problem."

I shook my head. "I don't think we should fly the ship over. They'd notice it too quickly and someone would go for help. Right now, we have the element of surprise," I said.

Wright nodded. "Good point, Baronette. We should formulate a plan to maximize it."

"I agree." I motioned some of the others closer. Marina came over, as did several of the commandos. We explained the situation to them and asked for input. After a round of ideas, Marina spoke up.

"We could try subterfuge," she said.

"What do you mean?" I asked.

"We could pose as Wyranth. Get them to open the gates to their facility willingly. Like we're going to pick up a supply of the stuff."

"I'm sure they have written orders or a code," Wright said.

Marina shrugged. "They might, but I was among them for a time. I've seen the serum pickups. I could fake being one of them well enough."

"It's not a bad idea," I said, "but we don't look like Wyranth soldiers."

Ethan stepped forward. "The knights engage in espionage missions like this from time to time. What we need to do is ambush a Wyranth group who's going to pick up the serum, and then take their uniforms. It's very doable. Great idea, Commander Willet."

Marina gave a half-bow.

"I like it," I said. "Lieutenant Willet, Ethan, First Sergeant Wright, Corporal Perry, Rhys, and Dr. du Clockhand, you'll form the second party. Bring a couple of other commandos for good measure. That's a small enough number not to be noticed in the plains and enough to be able to take on the Wyranth," I said.

"Excellent," Wright said. "We'll capture a Wyranth vehicle and send one of the commandos back to report to you when it's accomplished."

"No need," I said, finally having the confidence to stand up for what I wanted to do without equivocation. I smiled at him. "I'm coming with you."

At this point, I'd pulled this kind of stunt enough times that the crew didn't even protest. The look in Wright's eyes showed he understood there would be no swaying my determination. "Of course," he said.

I clasped my hands together. "Let's rest up, take the day to catch up on sleep, and head out at nightfall. Rislandia is relying on us."

CHAPTER 18

We caught those blasted Wyranth by surprise! The battle was ours today. Tomorrow, we advance and reclaim our lost territory.

An excerpt From Baron von Monocle's Log
Day 26 of the Month of Princesses
24th Year of King Malaky XV's Reign

WE LEFT AT dusk, but it was completely dark when we reached the place where our commandos had seen the Wyranth vehicle. We'd traveled for a long time off the main road, but followed a trail through the forest. Eventually, we stopped and stood to the side of the worn trail.

"Do we wait for one of them to come down the road and try to jump on their vehicle?" I asked. The prospect didn't sound like the best plan. We probably should have gone over these details hours before, but with no Wyranth around, now was as good as any time to figure out what to do when they did arrive.

"We can do one better than that," First Sergeant Wright said. He motioned to one of his commandos. "Krueger, get over here and open your pack," he said.

Krueger removed his pack from his back. The commandos carried much bigger packs than I did, and I was glad to not have to come up through those ranks and haul such weight. I would have toppled over from exhaustion if I did. Once the pack was open, Krueger produced an ax.

"Ah, I see," Ethan said, grinning. "We make them stop. A much less risky proposition."

Krueger moved over to a nearby tree and chopped at its trunk. His fellow commandos started to tease him about the work he had to do. First Sergeant Wright responded by making them rotate duties hacking at the tree, which brought about groans from the other two commandos. They went to work despite their protests. It wasn't long before the trunk's structure couldn't hold its weight any longer. The bottom of the tree made a crackling noise.

"Everybody back," Corporal Perry said.

We backed away from the tree as the noises grew louder. The tree bent toward the road and, suddenly, the entire weight of it came collapsing down in a crash. It kicked up dust along the road, leaves gently floating through the air.

Despite not being close to the crash, I found myself cringing.

Ethan chuckled at me. "Fearless adventurer, undone by a tree falling."

I wrinkled my nose at him but couldn't actually be mad. A little humor and teasing never hurt anyone, though I would have to get him back later. I laughed along with him.

The tree landed squarely in the middle of the road, just as the commandos wanted. My team circled it to make sure there wouldn't be an easy way for the Wyranth to circumvent it. Determining they needed a slightly better location, the men rolled it over until some bushes and rocks would make it impossible to drive around.

After the tree was in place, we moved to the side of the road into an inconspicuous location where we could maintain cover.

"We should probably get some sleep," I said. Even though we'd taken a rest before heading out, I was still tired from staying up for more than a day during the last battle. I wanted to keep my wits fresh when we came across Wyranth the next time.

"I agree," Dr. du Clockhand said. "It's been a long couple of days."

Wright nodded. "Let's make camp in the trees over there." He pointed to a place several yards from the road. An extra precaution so we wouldn't risk being discovered. "No fires so we don't draw any attention, and we'll rotate watch. Corporal Perry, you take the first," he said.

The commandos spread out bedrolls and, soon, we were ready to get a little rest. Marina and I laid down first. I hadn't been on any overnight missions in the woods, so I wasn't used to the hard ground. But If I could sleep with the loud noises the airship turbines made, and the way the ship rocked with turbulence, I shouldn't have any trouble here.

The world faded before I could form another thought. I dreamed of being in the Wyranth dungeon, tugging on the bars relentlessly, trying to escape even though I had no means to do so. I was screaming and crying. All I wanted was my father, but he had disappeared. No guards ever came in the dungeon. Wouldn't they feed me? Or give me something to drink?

It went on like that for a long time before someone shook me awake. I'd almost forgotten that wasn't the reality. "Leave me alone," I mumbled.

"Zaira," a soft, masculine voice said. "The Wyranth are here. We need you up."

Ethan. He needed me. I quickly sat up and nearly collided heads with him in the process. My eyes adjusted to my surroundings. I wasn't in a prison. I was in the forest. We had a mission to perform. "Oh," I said, coming to alertness and shaking the weariness off.

Ethan laughed, though he still kept his voice low. "You're funny when you wake up." He offered a hand to me. "Come on."

I let him help me to my feet and saw the others waking up around me. It must have been Ethan's watch when the Wyranth came.

Everyone understood what we needed to do and where we needed to go. We moved quietly toward the road, as careful with our footsteps as we were quick. It was still dark out, making it hard to see in front of us, but the Wyranth vehicle's headlights pointed at the tree trunk in the middle of the road, illuminating the general area. Three Wyranth soldiers had gotten out of the vehicle to try to move it. The vehicle itself was fairly large, with a tarp-covered back and a steamstack protruding from the middle of it, blasting steam into the air. The motor ran and made a loud *clackety* noise as its gears turned over.

We outnumbered the Wyranth, but we still had to be careful. These were men under the influence of the serum. It would make them crazed, unable to stop fighting. It would be difficult to take prisoners, and we couldn't allow any to escape and warn others about our presence here. We also wanted to keep their uniforms intact. This had to go perfectly.

Before I could complete my thought, several pistol shots rang out. The Wyranth who were out of the car turned and fell. To my right, the commandos stood, guns smoking. They hadn't hesitated.

I brought my hand to my chest, shocked at the way they executed those soldiers. This was war, and I had seen a lot of grave sights, but the sheer cold-bloodedness of their actions made me nauseous.

We still had a fourth Wyranth to deal with. He exited the vehicle from the driver's side to see what happened. Ethan grabbed him by the shirt, slamming the hilt of his sword into the Wyranth's face. The driver collapsed to the ground. "I think that's the last of them!" Ethan said. He'd moved so quickly around the vehicle, I'd hardly noticed. The knights were incredible to watch in action.

The others set to work stripping the Wyranth of their uniforms, and we compared sizes to see who received one. None of them fit my shorter frame, which disappointed me, but I didn't need to be part of the party sneaking their way in. I could hide in the back with those of us who didn't have uniforms. While the others dressed, I moved around to the back of the vehicle. The tarp covered a large bed in the back where several people could lay down inconspicuously.

"Everyone outside of Wyranth uniform to the back of this truck," I said. "We don't need to split our party. We can hide in here while our more visible group infiltrates." When I turned back, Ethan, Wright, Perry, and Kruger had Wyranth uniforms on. They weren't perfect fits, but I couldn't see any blood or tears in the fabric.

Ethan dragged the driver out in front of everyone. "We should probably get rid of him," he said.

He meant to kill a helpless man. I knew it was our enemy, and his escape would mean trouble for us, but I couldn't go along with that. It was against everything we stood for. "There has to be another way," I said.

Rhys stepped forward. "If you wouldn't mind trying something, I could use a subject to see if my counter-serum works. I've been developing it since we arrived from my home continent, and though I don't have many samples, it sounds like we're going to be entering a facility where I could replicate it for mass consumption."

"Do it," I said.

Rhys gathered his things and set them down beside the unconscious Wyranth. The others set to work rolling the tree trunk away so we could take the vehicle down the dirt road unencumbered. I watched the others work, hands on my hips. *Managing*, as my father would put it.

Dr. du Clockhand squatted beside Rhys and revived the Wyranth with smelling salts when he was ready. Immediately, the Wyranth thrashed on the ground, trying to free himself from his Rislandian captors.

"Oops," Rhys said. "I should have injected him first. A little help here!"

The Wyranth clawed at Rhys, pulling him forward by the shirt. Rhys went wide-eyed in surprise, dropping the syringe. Our commandos saw the interchange and hurried over, but the Wyranth managed to grab the syringe. He jabbed the needle at Rhys, who narrowly avoided getting stabbed. Corporal Perry arrived soon after and grabbed the Wyranth's arm, able to hold his hand back. The force of his grip caused the Wyranth to lose hold of the syringe. Rhys quickly scooped it out of the dirt.

"Keep him still," Rhys said.

The Wyranth kept squirming, but between our commandos and Dr. du Clockhand, he couldn't slip from their grasps. Rhys moved to a place by the man's head and jabbed the syringe into his neck. The Wyranth's eyes went wide, and he howled with pain, continuing to resist. Once the serum was inside of him, Rhys removed the needle and scrambled to his feet, stepping away from the crazed man.

"How fast will this work?" I asked

"The serum I used on Marina took only a few minutes, but she was in withdrawal and not actively ingesting the original agent. I'm not certain," he said. "This is also somewhat more potent. It should have a calming effect."

Several minutes passed while the Wyranth fought my men's grips on him.

"We need to get going soon," Ethan said. "We don't want to waste the darkness of night."

Concealment was of utmost importance for us, especially if we were going to sneak our whole team into this Wyranth operation. But it was worth the wait trying to see if this serum did its trick.

The Wyranth seemed to fight a little less as time wore on. Perhaps he was getting tired, or it may have been the serum, it was impossible to tell. Then he went limp.

"Is he dead?" I asked.

Dr. du Clockhand placed two fingers on his wrist. "No, there's a pulse."

"He's coming back to," Rhys said.

The Wyranth blinked several times, but he didn't resist the soldiers holding his limbs down any longer. "Wh... where am I?"

"You're in Rislandian territory," Corporal Perry said, his tone chastising.

"Oh, right," the Wyranth said, sounding contrite. "On a mission with my unit. I remember now."

"Let him up," Rhys said, talking to the commandos.

Wright looked at me for confirmation. I nodded. The commandos released the Wyranth, allowing him to sit up on his own. "You're the enemy," the Wyranth said, sounding confused. With a few of us in Wyranth uniforms, it must have been a strange sight.

"We've spared your life," Ethan said, standing and keeping his hand on the hilt of his sword.

The Wyranth seemed to consider this for a moment. "Yes, you did," he said. "I've no interest in fighting you."

"Of course he'd say that," Perry said. "He's surrounded by us."

I stepped forward, ignoring Perry's concerns. "If we were to let you go, you would have to swear not to tell others of our presence here. Can you do that?"

"I would return home, to my land. It's been too long since I've seen my family," the soldier said. Whether he meant it or not, I couldn't tell, but he sounded sincere.

"I believe it worked," Rhys said.

"Can't trust a Wyranth," Perry said.

It wasn't as if Perry were being unreasonable. It was a risk to let him go. I could tell by the look Ethan gave me that he didn't like the idea. On the other hand, the counter-serum clearly worked. I'd seen the sheer rage the Wyranth operated under when they were under the influence of the giant's blood concoction. This man no longer had the violent look in his eyes.

"We'll let you go," I said. "You'll have to head this way." I pointed in the direction of the road behind the vehicle. "If we see you again on this path, we won't have any mercy."

"Thank you," the Wyranth said, clearly relieved. He pushed himself to his feet.

I stepped to the side. The others didn't move. After a time, the Wyranth walked by me and hurried off away from us.

Once he was gone, my people relaxed.

"I don't like it," Ethan said.

"Neither do I," Perry agreed.

Rhys picked his bag off the ground. He beamed with pride. "This concoction works far better than what I'd given Marina before. You see, what I'd done was nullify the effects. This actively sends the opposite signal to the man affected, in addition to removing the addiction. I believe it worked well." He smiled. "For the next two to three days, at least, our Wyranth friend will be a pacifist."

"Which should buy us the time we need, if that's true," Wright said.

"Great," I said, trying to sound cheerful. "Let's get going before he realizes he should warn the people at the mine."

There was no more argument. What was done was done, and though the commandos and Ethan didn't agree with my decision, they weren't going to question me. It felt like I was really settling into command. I had to do things a little differently, treating people with compassion and dignity, even if they were the enemy. We had to remember who we were, which was better than the Wyranth in their monster blood-addled states of mind.

We piled into the vehicle, the four of my men in Wyranth uniforms up front, the rest of us under the tarps in the back. Ethan revved the engine, and we began moving down the bumpy dirt trail.

CHAPTER 19

The battle for Desert Watch lasted three days. The airship wasn't much help here, as we couldn't drop cannonballs on to our own city. These last several days have been bloody, but we finally have the area secure. We can rebuild what the Wyranth destroyed.

An excerpt From Baron von Monocle's Log
Day 30 of the Month of Princesses
24th Year of King Malaky XV's Reign

WE ARRIVED AT the mine a little over an hour later. Ethan drove a little too fast for my liking. The bumps in the trail made us slip and slide all over the back of the Wyranth vehicle. The others laughed about the rough ride at first, but it grated on them over time as the bumps in the road made our backs ache. Soon enough, everyone complained about their discomfort.

When we arrived, we made sure we were out of sight, covering ourselves with tarps we found in the back and using some of the Wyranth's supply crates to obscure us further. If the Wyranth wanted to look in here, they wouldn't see us. At least we hoped they wouldn't.

The sound of boots on gravel approached our vehicle. "I haven't seen you before," a man said.

"Lots of casualties on the front lines. They sent me to bring back a fresh supply of the serum," Ethan said. His voice was calm. He lied almost *too* well for my comfort. Even when my father had pretended to be a Wyranth soldier in my presence, I'd noticed a hesitancy in his voice. Ethan had none.

"A lot of new people are coming through," another male voice said, slightly more distant. "Let them pass. If they're late on their supply, the whole advance could break down."

The first male voice grumbled his agreement.

Ethan restarted the engine, and we moved forward again. None of us in the back of the vehicle dared move. There might be another checkpoint or something we couldn't be certain about. The road was a little bumpier than before, but we also drove more slowly.

The vehicle stopped again. I wished I could see anything other than the tarp over our heads. This time, Ethan opened the door to the car. His feet fell on the ground by the driver's side.

"Here for a serum supply? How many troops are you accountable for?" someone asked him.

"Uh..." Ethan paused. "About a thousand."

"They're really cranking out the supplies from here. I'm not sure we'll be able to keep up production if this goes on for much longer," the voice said.

The other doors opened. More footsteps. All of our Wyranth-clad men had moved from the vehicle. A gun *clicked*.

"Wait... what are you doing?" the voice said.

A gunshot blasted.

I winced, imagining an unarmed, helpless man being shot. We had to clear this area of Wyranth, but couldn't they have used Rhys's trick on the Wyranth soldier we did in the forest? No, there were too many of them here. Too much risk.

More gunshots fired.

"Alright, time to get out and join us. Jig's up," Ethan said. "We're in a fairly defensible position."

We pushed the tarp off, and Rhys moved the boxes at the back of the bed away so we could make our way out the back. He was the first out, with our other commando following close behind.

They helped us three women down, and by the time they did, more Wyranth had arrived.

I surveyed my surroundings. We were behind several crates, which, along with the vehicle, provided us with some cover. There was a large pit with several mechanical pipes, just like I had seen back in Devil's Mountain, behind the Wyranth capital. A large wooden rope bridge was overhead us, and we appeared to be in a room dug out of a hill. There was one large entrance to allow vehicles in and some further digging out back.

Like the pit from before, the cavern glowed. It was one of the giant creatures. When I'd last encountered one of these creatures, I could feel the creature tugging at my mind from a small dose of the serum I'd ingested. This time, I felt nothing, for which I was grateful. It could be that the serum developed from its blood created a bond with a specific giant. I was no scientist, but I tucked away the thought. At some point, I could talk to Rhys about it.

Ethan and the commandos fired their guns toward the approaching Wyranth. Four of them were in coveralls, worker garb, but three others were in uniform. Corporal Perry told us there'd been about twenty people here, and this accounted for nine, plus the two guards we encountered out front. It was the middle of the night, so it made sense that some of the others wouldn't be around. We were lucky.

The first round of gunfire took down three of the workers and one of the soldiers, but it alerted the others to where we were. The remaining Wyranth scuttled for cover. The last worker scrambled on the ground for the downed soldier's weapon. Before he could reach it, Marina had leveled her gun and shot him. It left us two soldiers to deal with.

"You're outnumbered!" First Sergeant Wright shouted. "Drop your guns and surrender!"

While he spoke, he motioned the others to take positions behind the boxes. I hid behind the vehicle with the other women and Rhys.

The Wyranth only responded by firing.

"So much for diplomacy," Ethan said.

I decided to circle around back and motioned to Marina to come with me. We made our way closer to the pit. This one had no rails, freshly formed. Inside lay a bubbling blob, with several veins at the surface of its gooey skin. Bright blue liquid coursed through it.

"Disgusting," Marina said.

"I know it," I said, ducking so the glowing light it radiated wouldn't make me a big target in the middle of the room. Marina did the same.

Several more shots were fired from each side. The Wyranth kept their focus on Ethan and the commandos. The boys were providing an excellent distraction, whether they'd intended to or not. Excitement coursed through me. I loved getting in on the action. It made me smile as I hurried across the edge of the pit and to the crates opposite. Once there, I stopped behind one of them, waiting for Marina to crouch next to me.

She grinned at me.

We both nodded to each other and proceeded forward. The firefight on the other side would keep going until one side ran out of bullets. I peeked my head up over the crate. The two Wyranth were crouched, focusing in the opposite direction. We had clear shots.

I pulled my pistol from its holster and used my free hand to lift my fingers and made numbers. One. Two. Three.

Both Marina and I stood over the boxes, leveling our guns at the two Wyranth soldiers. We fired, and from this close of a range, it was easy to connect with our targets. They fell over in pain. We fired again. It was all too easy, but we ducked back down in case there was a little bit of fight left in them.

After a few more moments, only silence came from their location. "They're down, Ethan! Hold your fire!"

"Zaira?" Ethan asked in surprise.

Marina and I stood again, and our team came out from their hiding places on the other side. I waved to Ethan. "Thanks for keeping them busy."

Ethan laughed. "No problem. Now what?"

"Now we secure the entrance and ensure those others don't get in here," Wright said. "Perry, hold the main entrance with our knight friend here. I'll circle around and make sure there's not more back doors to this place."

"Yes, sir," Perry said, moving into a position to guard the large opening at the front of the cavern. Marina joined the two at the entrance.

Krueger moved the fallen soldiers to a central location and patted down their bodies. He produced some papers from one of the Wyranth and brought them to Wright. "Look at this," he said.

First Sergeant Wright took the papers and scrutinized them. Krueger grabbed a lantern and held it up to help him be able to read.

"These are in code," Wright said. "We'll have to have someone decipher them when we get a chance. Good work, Corporal."

Krueger nodded and resumed his cleanup of our area.

Dr. du Clockhand and Rhys carefully moved from the cover of the Wyranth vehicle, glancing around the cavern. "This is quite a laboratory," Rhys said. "Nearly as advanced as some of the equipment I was working with in the Nightmen city." He moved over to a metal contraption by the large blob pit. It had a number of gauges, gears, and pipes protruding from it, and it looked to be in its *off* position. Adjacent to it was a table with several glass containers and scientific instruments. Rhys ran his finger over what looked to be a control board, and then found a knob to twist.

The device shook, and I heard the sound of gears grinding against each other inside of it. The table beside it turned into a conveyor, and the device spat out the blue giant's blood into vials. An arm dropped down for each one, putting a cork stopper into the vials. The mechanics were incredible. Steam filled the room.

"Well then," Rhys said. "It looks like I'll have all the supply I'll need to make an anti-serum. I wonder if this contraption could be rigged to add my solutions. If we can produce it as quickly as this blood churns out, I think we might be able to come up with a solution to our Wyranth problem."

"Can you do... whatever it is you need to do?" I asked, gesturing toward the machine.

Rhys shook his head. "I'd need an engi—"

Before he could complete his sentence, a bullet whizzed by my head. The shot echoed through the chamber.

I ducked. So did Rhys.

Perry came running through the cave mouth. "Incoming!"

At the entrance to the cave stood four Wyranth soldiers. They pressed forward, guns pointed toward us. Perry, Krueger, Ethan, and Marina used the entrance of the cave for cover. They returned fire at the Wyranth. One went down, making a gurgling noise.

In my crouch, I moved as quickly as I could to get one of the crates between me and the Wyranth soldiers. More gunfire came from both sides. It seemed my life was a revolving door of gun battles lately. The initial thrill of the action was beginning to wane. Now I found these battles wearing on me.

After a volley of Wyranth shots, I peeked my head over the crate, pointing my pistol toward the entrance. I pulled the trigger and ducked again. I heard another Wyranth soldier yelp in pain. I got one. That made two so far. In some ways, it made me wish James were here. We might have made a competition of who could do the most damage to the Wyranth soldiers. I found myself missing him, even in the heat of the battle.

The rest of our team rushed over from the back door then, guns blazing as they pushed forward. The chamber filled with so much gunfire it all seemed to blend together, and then it stopped, dust everywhere. The machine in the background was still cranking giant's blood into vials on the conveyor, making its noises as it putted along and produced more steam.

I slowly stood, peering into the dusty scene in front of me. The four Wyranth all lay dead on the ground. My team moved closer to them.

Wright's forehead wrinkled when he frowned. "There's still five or so more of them out there, and they know we're here. I'd venture to guess they went to get backup, since they didn't come with these folks. We're going to need a larger contingent to keep this facility secure. I'd also like to see if we can't find someone to decipher the coded message the Wyranth had on him." He turned to me. "Unless we're going to blow the place and leave."

"No!" Dr. du Clockhand protested. "Rhys has the ability to produce a cure. We all saw it work on that one soldier. That's how we're going to save Rislandia, not by cutting off their supply and having mad soldiers roaming our countryside."

"I would be inclined to agree," Rhys said.

I holstered my pistol and turned to Rhys. "You said you needed an engineer to help you with the machine here?"

Rhys nodded, moving to the machine and stopping its assembly line by twisting a knob on the control board. "Yes, or a team of them."

"I bet Harkerpal would be able to whip you up what you need," I said, grinning. He would be thrilled to have a challenging project.

"Except he's back on the airship," Wright said.

"We can't send up a flare here, since we don't know how many Wyranth are in the immediate area, and we don't want to draw too much attention to us. Who's our fastest runner?" I said, glancing around to the whole team.

Ethan sighed. "Probably me. Our knight training prepares us for courier duty in desperate situations."

I nodded. "There we have it. You'll go to the *Liliana*. Tell Lieutenant Colwell they'll need to take off and come to the mine. It'll solve both of our problems. They'll be able to spot Wyranth backup from above and provide defense. And we'll get Harkerpal and his team to help with the machine so we can mass produce Rhys' anti-serum." I clasped my hands together, proud of my idea.

Ethan handed First Sergeant Wright his sword. "Hold this for me and be careful with it."

Wright grunted an agreement. Ethan took off running.

CHAPTER 20

We had thought the battle was over, but another force of Wyranth are on the way up from the desert. How did such a large army cross through such a desolate land?

An excerpt From Baron von Monocle's Log
Day 34 of the Month of Princesses
24th Year of King Malaky XV's Reign

ETHAN RETURNED VIA airship several hours later, dropping to the front of the mine on a rope ladder. Even though I was still inside the cavern with the strange giant blob monster, I felt secure knowing the *Liliana* was circling above us. Rhys and Harkerpal got to work at once on the device, conscripting several of Harkerpal's junior engineers to do much of the manual labor. Thanks to our well-stocked engine room, they had all the tools they needed to weld together new metal bits and parts into working machinery.

Several of our people on the ship took stabs at deciphering the Wyranth coded message, as well. Most had no idea what they were looking at and didn't try to decode the message. Major Ral said he thought he figured out part of it and would like to take the papers for further study. Maybe his pilot brain could figure out some patterns others couldn't.

For the first time in several days, I had a break to sit and think, as did the other commandos. I never realized how much of a luxury it could be to not be fighting. We'd faced so much battle, everything had been a blur, with very little time to think about anything.

I wondered how James was faring with King Malaky and Princess Reina at their retreat. The location was so secluded it was fairly safe from Wyranth soldiers marching, but I would have thought Rislandia City would be too far north from them to ever reach. Nothing was safe unless we could turn the tide.

If Rhys's work could make them stop fighting, even for a few days, we had a chance.

I returned to the airship to write my logs, check on the crew, and ensure our supplies were strong. We were low on cannonballs, but the ship had several weeks' worth of supplies if we desperately needed it. If worst comes to worst, we could flee to Atrebla or beyond and not need to set down for some time. I hoped it wouldn't come to that.

The next three days went by slowly, even as we anxiously waited for the Wyranth's backup to arrive. I did my patrols of the ship, checked on everyone. The crew was less on edge than they had been, but there was still a sense of dread and worry overwhelming everyone. I wasn't sure what to do about it. Should I give a speech?

By all accounts, Rhys's work was going well, and faster than anticipated. He knew what he needed. His original anti-serum had worked with the one soldier. It was just a matter of mass-replicating the cure. We would have to find a way to distribute it to everyone still, but if we had the cure, we could figure that out when the time came.

Major Ral thought he cracked some of the code. He said the top lines of the papers said "Project Walking Monster," which he believed could be something regarding Wyranth troop deployments. It would make sense. If it were true, we needed the information sooner rather than later.

I went about writing down what I hoped would be an inspiring speech to deliver to the crew. After several starts and stops, I was finally getting a flow in my writing. There was hope for Rislandia. We were the hope of Rislandia. It was on us to keep the fight alive, to keep the spirit of our great kingdom going. Even as I wrote the words, hope stirred within me. This was going to be good.

A knock came at the door of my quarters. I looked up, and Toby peeked his little head out from under my bed out of curiosity.

"You going to answer that?" I asked my ferret.

He chirped.

I laughed and set my pen down. "Come on in," I said more loudly.

The door opened. Ethan stood there. "Hey. Seeing how you're holding up," he said.

"As well as can be, I suppose. Trying to write a speech to get the crew motivated. You?"

"Hanging in there," Ethan said with a smile. It was different than his usual smile, a little more forced.

"Want to talk about something?"

Ethan shrugged. "I was more hoping you'd come to the deck with me to watch the sunset."

A soft tingle ran through me from my stomach all the way up to my throat. It was as if I lost all the weight in my body and I was going to float off the floor. I tried to compose myself as I stood and forgot all about the speech. "Yes, I think that would be delightful," I said. It came off sounding mechanical.

"You're funny when you try to sound like a proper lady," Ethan said.

I narrowed my eyes at him. "What's that supposed to mean?"

Ethan laughed. "Nothing, just that I should be a proper gentleman." He held the door for me, and I exited my quarters.

I waited for him to step beside me, and he offered his arm.

Though I was still technically on duty as the commander of the airship, we were taking a break, right? It wasn't as if the crew were unaware of our... mutual interest in each other. I'd heard enough snickers, and Marina certainly ribbed me about it every chance she got. Like she was any better with her beau, Rhys. I swear, if I found them kissing in public again I'd whack her upside the head.

My hesitation caused the confidence to disappear from Ethan's eyes. He was so easily hurt by my actions. I had to be more careful. So, I made the next move, reaching my hand out and curling my fingers around his bicep. It was hard and muscular, and the sensation of the touch stilled my breath. It was getting too hot in here. I couldn't wait for the breeze from the airship deck.

We walked along together until we reached the door to the deck, when Ethan held it for me again. Out on the deck, Ethan didn't offer an arm, but took my hand, his fingers intertwining with mine.

One of the deckhands whistled at us.

My lips tightened together as I turned to angrily address the peeping Tom...

"Ignore him," Ethan said, tugging me along in the opposite direction.

Without a choice given to me, I stumbled until I regained my footing and we stepped toward the railing. The sun was just setting over the western horizon. The forest disappeared into the skyline, and the world was filled with a brilliant red-pink coloration.

"I read once that when the sky is this red, it's because a volcano erupted somewhere in the world. It's the sunlight reflecting off the smoke in the air," Ethan said.

"I believe it," I said. "Though I'd be content to never see a volcano again."

"Me too," Ethan said.

We stood, watching the bright orange sun slip below the horizon until it was just a tiny speck of light in a darkening sky. The reddish colors washed into purples, and shadows fell across the forest below us.

After a while, Ethan sighed. "I'm worried about my family," he said.

"Oh?" I hadn't heard him talk much about his family before. I knew his father was a lord of a fishing village. Where did he say he was from again? I felt bad for not recalling."Shellville, right?" I asked, guessing.

Ethan nodded. "Which is south on the road, just after Portsgate."

I understood suddenly why he wasn't quite himself. Though he hid it well—as a strong knight he was trained to keep his emotions at bay—he was hurting. Portsgate had been razed to the ground by the Wyranth. It meant Shellville was likely in similar disrepair. Which meant his family might not be alive anymore.

"My father always lectured me about studying, told me if I was to inherit the holdings someday, I needed to learn as much as I could so I could understand the concerns of our people and make wise decisions on their behalf. It's a morbid thing to think about, but I don't want to inherit his lands or titles." His voice sounded shaky for the first time I could recall.

"I'm sorry, Ethan. Maybe he's okay? Once we're out of this mess, we'll use the ship to go look for your family." Did he have brothers and sisters? I was an only child, but I knew so little about him. It didn't seem the time to ask, however. It would only worry him more.

"That's very kind of you," he said, turning to me.

I looked into his eyes. He was taller than me. We were so close now, and it was becoming dark. He wrapped his arms around me. It wasn't like the last time, when I was surprised by his kiss. This time, he didn't make a motion on that front, but he seemed to be holding me for his own support. I was happy to give it to him. I didn't know what to say to make it better, but I didn't want him to hurt. I wrapped my arms around his waist and held him close. We stood there for a long time, quiet, together. It felt so right and so natural. How had I missed out on something like this for all my years? I never wanted to move from here.

"Wyranth!" One of the deckhands shouted, breaking the mood immediately.

Ethan backed away from me and looked out over the rails.

Out beyond the forest, a large contingent of Wyranth marched in our direction. It was mostly infantry, and judging from the distance, we would have an hour or two to prepare for them.

We'd done significant damage to their vehicles and fighting contraptions, but there were enough that they would certainly overwhelm our people below.

I turned to Ethan. "I need you to go down and warn the others. We need to pack up what we can." The implications were staggering. We had to do something about the facility below. The Wyranth couldn't be allowed to regain control over it.

"And make sure we destroy anything we leave behind," Ethan finished my thought. He nodded. "Got it."

"Be careful too, okay?" I asked, eyes searching his.

Ethan smiled, more earnest this time. "I will." With that, he turned and made his way for the rope ladder.

I made for the bridge. Lieutenant Colwell and Major Ral were ready at their stations. "Orders?"

"We're going to try to slow those Wyranth down," I said. "I wish we still had any of those explosive shells."

"We've always done well with cannonballs before," Colwell said.

And we were growing low on those, as well. How many more battles could we have without resupplying? The airship would be useless once we ran out. It was something I couldn't worry about. We had to do what we could for now.

Turning to look out the window onto the deck, I nodded to strengthen my resolve. "Let's show them what we're made of. For steam and country."

"For steam and country," the two men repeated. Without the roar of the crew saying it, it didn't sound as confident as I would have liked, but we had to retain our traditions and keep our sense of selves as Rislandians. That's what this fight was all about. What we would die for if we had to.

CHAPTER 21

There's too many of them, even with the airship in the skies and our Grand Rislandian Army ready. We're going to have to come up with a new plan.

An excerpt From Baron von Monocle's Log
Day 34 of the Month of Princesses
24th Year of King Malaky XV's Reign

THE AIRSHIP LURCHED as it shifted from hovering to speeding forward. We needed to handle the Wyranth quickly and return to pick the rest of our people up. On the ground below, the treetops blurred together as we crossed the forest with incredible speed. Soon, we were nearly above the Wyranth soldiers.

I couldn't hear the shouts from below, but some of the Wyranth soldiers scattered. The sight of the *Liliana* inspired fear, and for good reason. Where we went, we wrecked their forces. And we would do so again.

Major Ral executed a hard turn of the airship that seemed all but impossible, banking the port cannons toward The Wyranth while we continued the same direction through the air. Our cannon blasts resounded, rattling the ship. I held onto the railing on the bridge, used to the jolting movements of the ship in battle. We flipped around again for the starboard cannons to do the same.

"That's the best we can do without using all of our ammunition. Bring us back to the mine, Major Ral. Let's hope it slowed them down," I said. We couldn't spend too much time here, and one volley should be enough to cause a disruption, at the very least. The ship spun about, making my stomach feel as if it were flying through my throat. I swallowed hard, trying to will the motion sickness away. Lieutenant Colwell's face had turned white.

"Sorry about that," Major Ral said. "That maneuver was a little over-zealous."

We sped back toward the mine, picking up a tail wind, which allowed us to move faster than we had on the way to face the Wyranth army. I looked behind us. Either we did significant damage to their forces or we didn't. Either way, we had to get our people to safety and get out of here.

Within minutes, we arrived back at the mine. Lieutenant Colwell looked through the telescope. "Our people are outside and ready. They look like they have a large crate with them. We'll have to send down extra rope to bring it aboard."

"Very good," I said.

Lieutenant Colwell motioned for me to go ahead, and both of us went out onto the deck to oversee the drops. From there, it was a matter of waiting as the commandos below secured our cargo, and the others migrated up the ropes and onto the ships.

Harkerpal was one of the first aboard, and he gave me an enthusiastic wave before padding over to me. "Baronette," he said.

"Harkerpal. How did everything go down there?"

"I was able to get the machinery up and running a few hours before the evacuation. Rhys would have liked some more time to produce extra formula, but we will make do with what we have. It reminds me of the time when there were five airships in the fleet. The skies were quite a terror for the enemy in those times." He bobbed his head as he talked, smiling to himself in the nostalgia of the moment.

Harkerpal continued, "We could hold these armies at bay with no problem if we had a fleet like we did in the old days. But even then, the ships had been in the air for so long we were running out of aether fuel, and your father brought the *Liliana* to swoop down into Rislandia City and pick up barrels of it via hooks. We had no time to stop or set down or the other ships would run out, and we dared not take them away from the battle supporting our other forces." He bobbed his head as he talked, smiling to himself in the nostalgia of the moment.

I wasn't sure the point of Harkerpal's story, but it was nice having him around. "I'm sure it was exciting. It's good to have you back aboard."

"Likewise. I should go check on my engines." He saluted me, something he rarely did. It was protocol to do so, of course, but I ran a fairly lax ship, as if we were family more than as if I were their commander. It felt strange to have these veteran soldiers saluting me. I supposed I was a veteran soldier now, too, but it still didn't feel like I deserved the salutes.

By the time he had spoken and departed, most of the others were aboard. First Sergeant Wright was the next to report to me, saluting as well.

I returned the gesture. "Are we ready to go?"

"I took the precaution of rigging the mine to explode yesterday. It seemed my planning was prudent," he said.

"Good work," I said. "How do we detonate—"

Before I could finish the sentence, a loud explosion rocked the area below us. It was loud enough to cause me to jump.

Wright suppressed a laugh by balling his fist and pressing it to his lips. "Oh, your face. I'm sorry, but it's hilarious."

I narrowed my eyes at him teasingly and flipped my hair over my shoulder. "Well, I suppose that's done. Has Rhys made it back aboard yet?"

"Present and accounted for," came a male voice beside me. When I turned to see him, Marina was holding his hand.

"I can't say I'm sad to blow that disgusting creature to bits," Marina said.

I understood her disdain for the giant. While I only had to deal with it seeping into my head for a few hours, Marina had lived with it pushing her actions into violence for weeks, and then months of withdrawal. "Hopefully, we secured enough of its blood to be able to make an impact."

Rhys sucked in his lower lip. "We were able to secure a good amount, but a lot less than I would have hoped. But after talking to Harkerpal, I believe we have a system of distribution that can create maximum impact. It's based on the way I'd seen some of the Nightmen manage their farms."

Farming was something I understood. I nodded. "Go on."

"Have you heard of crop dusting?"

"Can't say I have."

"It's taking an aerial device like the airship here and making a low pass to spread insecticide onto a large number of crops in a short time. It uses a chemical agent, much like our serum, combined with a thickener so it spreads out and isn't just a liquid. That's what I'd need to formulate to make my anti-serum spread across a greater area. Harkerpal says he would be able to assemble a spraying mechanism, and we simply shoot it from the bottom of the *Liliana's* hull."

It seemed to be a pretty good idea. I considered it. "You said fly low. That will be pretty difficult with a ship the size of the *Liliana*. It would give the Wyranth opportunities to blow holes in us," I said.

"No different than a number of other risks we take," Marina said.

"True, but I don't like to risk the entirety of the crew at once if I can help it." I glanced back to the bridge. "Major Ral will probably find the piloting challenge to be a fun one."

"It's just an idea for now," Rhys said. "Like I said, I need to figure out a thickening agent, and there's a lot to prepare for. I'll require a better laboratory than a small room aboard the ship."

I took that as a not-so-subtle hint. "We'll get to one." But would we? I glanced out over the side of the ships. We were on the move, but I hadn't given any particular directions to the crew yet.

We had to find somewhere to set down and formulate a better plan. I'd been so excited with the prospect of finding this giant the last few days that I hadn't really taken a moment to consider what to do next.

My hope was to have discovered something within the mine, kept it secure, and then distribute the serum as we were able.

This crop dusting idea sounded promising. Even if the image in my head of the *Liliana* dousing Wyranth soldiers with the anti-serum was amusing.

But the weight of these decisions didn't rest solely on me, as much as it often felt that way. It was a lot of pressure. I reached to rub the back of my neck.

"Where are we headed to next?" Marina asked.

"To get some ideas from people who are much more experienced at this than me," I said. "We're going to Cliffside Castle." With those words, I spun and headed for the bridge to give Major Ral the orders.

CHAPTER 22

A blizzard has fallen over southern Rislandia. Ice and snow are everywhere. At least the Wyranth won't be able to advance again toward Lake Bethany. It's bought us some time.

An excerpt From Baron von Monocle's Log
Day 10 of the Month of the Fool
24th Year of King Malaky XV's Reign

WE TOOK A route to Cliffside Castle that would have looked like a crescent shape on a map, almost backtracking to King's Retreat, but not crossing the mountains. We all agreed it wouldn't be prudent to encounter the bulk of the Wyranth forces while we were carrying a potential weapon against them without the means to deploy it. Which meant avoiding Rislandia City and any of their potential next targets if they continued their march.

The trip took most of the evening and into the next day as we looped around the northernmost part of our corner of the Areth continent. We turned west when we hit the ocean, traveling along the coast. It was rocky, the wind cold, and giant waves splashed against the shore. Once we came closer, the cliffs came into sight that gave Cliffside Castle its name. They stood tall from the water, even from our vantage. The port appeared next, with its series of long stairs and ramps that wound up the cliffs from the city.

Dozens of boats crowded into the docks at the port, from small yachts to bigger cargo vessels. They traveled around Rislandia and beyond to neighboring kingdoms, and with Portsgate and the south being under Wyranth control, many ships had nowhere else to go. Dock workers struggled to unload goods with mechanical, steam-powered cranes. Their exhausts shot into the air, dissipating before they reached our heights.

And then there was the castle itself. It was built out of elegant stone, polished by the cool saltwater air to create a smooth, shiny surface. The castle was beautiful, twin towers looming above everything else, not nearly the size of the spire, but impressive nonetheless.

Over the centuries, the settlement had sprawled out of the original castle walls, buildings and shops and people spread all along the cliffside. If matters with the Wyranth became any worse, those people might need the protection of the castle's fortifications.

"Set us down in the empty pasture by the road," I said, pointing to a place out the port window.

Major Ral craned his neck to take a look, and then went to work with the controls, pushing the levers into place.

The airship descended, the castle and city beyond growing in our view. A small procession marched down the main road, an honor guard of soldiers in Grand Rislandian Army grays. I lost sight of them as the ship landed. The *Liliana* swayed but didn't rock.

"One of your best landings, if I do say," Lieutenant Colwell said.

Major Ral grinned. "Set her down like a baby, I did."

"Good work," I said, nodding to the men before stepping out onto the deck. The crew worked their posts, tying down various pieces of equipment to ensure the proper landing procedures were in place.

I moved past them, my cape flowing behind me. It wasn't long before I arrived in the cargo bay. The crew were just opening the ramp to the outside. The ramp lowered, and Cliffside Castle's honor guard came into view, my father standing at the front. Scanning the eyes of the soldiers, I didn't see the optimism or will to fight that once characterized our army. We had all been so sure we were in the right and, as a consequence, we would prevail. But did the world care about morality? It seemed as if despite our best intentions, we kept failing. And didn't Ivan mention something about morality being worthless? The reminder of his comment unsettled me, but not as much as the sight of civilians' long faces shook me.

My father saluted.

I stepped down the ramp and returned the salute.

"Good to see you, Zaira," my father said, his hand dropping to his side.

"Likewise."

My father made a motion to the troops, who turned and marched back toward the castle proper. "We have a lot to discuss."

"That we do. Should I follow you?"

He nodded.

Our walk went quietly as we traveled the main road into the city. The streets were packed with people. Some lived in tents, and some looked like they were living on the streets without shelter. Several children ran in the streets, kicking a ball back and forth. Their hair was matted, their clothes wrinkled, but they still played. The parents didn't look nearly so joyous to be there.

Eyes followed us as we moved through the streets, only getting denser with people as we came closer to the castle. An overwhelming sense of dread overcame me. All of these people were counting on our efforts, and we weren't just failing ourselves, but we were failing them. It was almost too much weight for me. I wanted to break down and cry, but I couldn't. Not now.

My father led us around a side street where the crowd wasn't so thick. It had a small door into the castle rather than the large gate. The inside was teeming with military men. Several were in deep conversation, moving through the stone hallways. Unlike

Rislandia City's palace, the walls had no decoration. They were barren, old, and worn.

We arrived at a small chamber with a couple of chairs and a round table, which had maps and stacks of paper on it. A small gas lamp illuminated the room from the corner. My father motioned to one of the chairs. "As you can see, the situation here is not ideal."

"I'd say. I've never seen so many miserable people," I said, taking the seat he offered.

"Mmm," my father agreed, eyes shifting away. "A lot of refugees. People with nowhere to go. The Wyranth are liable to slaughter them, and there are very few places with food. We don't have the ability to sustain this city much longer as it stands. While we do have the port and fishing on the coast, we've lost most of the country's farmland. Supplies aren't coming in. Our supply master estimates we've got a week left before people will starve. We have to begin rations immediately."

It was worse than I'd ever anticipated. I couldn't imagine thousands of people starving. Plainsroad Village had been a place of plenty, where I was provided for, where crops grew with ease. The king ran the land well, and Rislandia City was downright decadent. It was so easy to go from having so much to having very little. It made me forget everything I'd come to talk to my father about. "What do we do?" I asked, my voice pleading.

"I do have some good news, if you can call it that."

"Yeah?"

"Talyen had our baby. We're naming her Lilly. You have a sister."

I wasn't expecting that at all. "Wow."

My father laughed. "Nothing else to say?"

"I mean, congratulations." It felt odd to congratulate him. I didn't know what to think. I'd been an only child my whole life. Though I knew Talyen was pregnant, I hadn't prepared myself to have a sister of all things. Not in the middle of this crisis.

What kind of life would she lead? Would she be on the run? Or worse, starving? It didn't seem fair to bring her into this world in the middle of our conflict. She couldn't have the stable life I did growing up. Though my father was away a lot, and my mother died young, I had support. What would she have?

"Something wrong?"

I realized I was frowning and tried to clear the expression off my face. "No, I'm just worried for her."

My father's eyes softened. "I am as well."

"Can I see her?" I asked.

"Soon," My father said, leaning back into his chair. "We have Talyen and her taken care of, I can promise that. But we need to discuss what we should do in the near future. Our forces have gathered here, our rallying point. Several contingents from the west and east have met us here. Our army is as strong as it will ever be. We took heavy casualties back in Rislandia City, but so did the Wyranth. The question is, do we retake the city, or do we wait here and make our stand?"

I considered for a moment, staring at the map, which was somewhat obscured by other papers. Cliffside Castle was in clear view, as was Rislandia City. It wasn't all that far. "I was just talking about this with my crew. We intercepted some Wyranth papers. It's coded, but Major Ral thinks there's something called 'Project Walking Monster' underway. I'm sure it has to do with their plans marching north... but that information's a few days old now."

I bit my lip, considering. "With this many people here, the Wyranth have to know how dire our situation is. Ivan, uh, the Iron Emperor, is a smart tactician. He'll understand he can wait us out and win without risking any more of his men."

"A fair point, and impressive uncovering a coded message," my father said. "When did you become so wise in the ways of war?"

I shrugged. "I've been in one."

He raised a curious brow at me. "And you said his name was Ivan. How did you find out his given name and when did you start calling him that?"

The question froze me. It was one I'd feared having to account for since I'd come back from my mission to the Zenwey continent.

A lump grew in my throat, and I tried to swallow. I could feel sweat beading beneath my blouse.

"You're not telling me something," my father said.

"I... I met with the Iron Emperor. He was here. Well, in Rislandia City. And again in Plainsroad Village."

"What?" My father's eyes went wide.

"He showed up in my apartment before the Zenwey mission. He was the one who convinced me to go. His troops were out of control. I don't think he lied to me."

My father's eyes turned cold. He looked angrier than I'd ever seen him. "This is unbelievable, Zaira. He was in our grasp and you didn't tell anyone? What were you thinking? What about the second time?"

"The first time, I thought we were doing both our kingdoms a favor. And we really did need to find a cure. The second, well, he told me he had snipers all around us. There was nothing I could do."

"By Malaky, I don't even know how to handle this. What you're talking about is treason. After he held us in his camp?"

"You're not even listening to me!" I slammed my hand on the table.

My father's jaw clamped shut. I could tell he wanted to yell back at me, but for the time being, he was going to listen. I had to seize the opportunity.

"I feel terrible about it already. Each and every person in those streets, it weighs on me," I said, pointing to my chest. My hand shook. "But it's irrational. I know what you're thinking. I took the airship out of commission for a long time. Because of that, we didn't have an aerial support when we needed it the most. I've thought about that every night since we've returned, and trust me, I lose sleep over it."

I paused to take a breath. "But by the same token, what if we were here? We're only one ship. We can't be everywhere in the kingdom all at once. The Wyranth would have still overrun us. And who knows, we might have lost the airship in the process.

145

Now we have a way to at least turn the tides, but I need you to listen and not be mad at me over a little mistake."

Silence hung in the air between us as we locked eyes. It was the first time I could remember challenging my father. He still didn't look any too pleased with me. "You had him in your grasp."

"He would have been long gone before I was able to rouse anyone at the palace. And how many people even know what he looks like?"

It took him a moment to process, but my father finally nodded. "You're right. And what's done is done. But still, you can't hide things from me. If I would have known the Iron Emperor himself was in our land and that our security was that lax..."

"We'd have the same result. You tried your best. So did I." As I said those words, I finally began to believe them. It was like a weight lifted from my shoulders. I hated having a secret, but in truth, there had been little I could do about the situation at the time.

"The second time, it was on this last excursion of yours?"

I nodded.

"He must be bold if he's pushing north with his army. He's not one to be overconfident either. This bodes ill for us," my father said, the tension evaporating from his face. "I'm sorry I was stern with you, Zaira."

"I'm sorry I was too scared to tell you," I said, casting my eyes aside, "but we have to move forward. Whatever he's planning, we have to counter it quickly."

"What do you have for me?"

I told him how Rhys hadn't just developed a cure for the Wyranth soldiers' withdrawals, but an anti-serum that caused people to lose their will to fight. The last few days were a blur, but I tried to recount every detail. I wouldn't make the mistake of leaving something out when talking to my father again. He needed to know everything in order to form the proper strategy for the army. "He said he needs a better laboratory to complete his work, and I was hoping he could find somewhere here to use. Though it seems space is at a premium."

When I'd finished telling him the story, he tapped his fingers on the table. "This is the best news I've heard in a while. Given our situation with the food, I think we should plan to advance on Rislandia City once Harkerpal's finished with adapting the *Liliana* to become... what did you call it?"

"A crop duster."

"Indeed."

"And we need to make sure Rhys has finished doing what he needs to do with his anti-serum," I reminded him.

The wheels turned in my father's mind, but it didn't seem like he was thinking of a place to put Rhys. When he had a plan, it was impossible to hold him back. The way his eyes scanned the map on the table beside us told me there was no deterring him.

"We'll need to lure them out of the city to the north. Not so far that we are in danger here, but in the open. That will be the best way to implement this strategy."

"How do we do that?" I asked.

My father considered for a moment, and then snapped his fingers. "Our food crisis. We can spread rumors about how bad it really is, and since we know they've been spying on us, we can leak that a major food shipment is going to be coming along the main road, about halfway between Rislandia City and here. It will draw them out because they'll think they can stop us, and they'll be greeted by the full force of the Rislandian Grand Army and, of course, the *Liliana*."

I grinned. "Sounds like a good idea."

"Excellent." My father stood. "For now..." he paused, frowning as he considered logistics. "You said your friend needed a lab, yes?"

"That's right," I said, standing along with him.

"We can set him up in the town's hospital. It won't be as good as some of the scientific research labs back in Rislandia City, but they should have better equipment than anywhere else. There's some sort of disease among the civilian refugees, but they're not too crowded at the moment."

"Sounds good. There's one more thing," I said.

"What's that?" my father asked.

"When we were back in Plainsroad Village, we found a journal. It had airship designs in it."

My father's eyes went wide. "I'd thought that was lost."

"It's found now."

"Keep that safe, Zaira. There's designs in there not just to recreate ships like the *Liliana* but also for personal aircraft. Once we have the city stabilized again..." He shook his head. "No, I'm getting ahead of myself. We have to win these battles first. Regardless, that book can be the key to the future." He moved toward the door. "I'll summon one of the apprentice knights to go fetch Rhys and take him to the hospital, and we'll set you up with a room here. I'm sure these last few days have been hard on you. You'll want to take a load off and get clean, no doubt."

"Do I smell that bad?" I asked.

My father laughed as he bounded into the hallway. "You smell worse than your pet ferret."

"Hey!" I said, laughing. It felt good to have some humor again. And it also felt good to have some hope. And a plan.

We turned the corner and met with two soldiers. My father relayed their orders and took me up a winding stone staircase to one of the castle towers, where he said I could stay. There were baths on the first floor and all I had to do was tell the servants when I was ready. "I'm going to meet with some of my officers and tell them the plan. We need to work out the details of the troop movements," my father said. "Then I'll come fetch you."

"For what?" I asked.

"To meet your sister, of course!"

CHAPTER 23

It's nice to be with Liliana again, even with the weight of the war in the south looming on me. I could only imagine having a family and being trapped away from her. I'm blessed to have an airship.

An excerpt From Baron von Monocle's Log
Day 11 of the Month of the Fool
24th Year of King Malaky XV's Reign

A SOAK IN the tub did me a lot of good. All of the weight and pressure melted away. My body finally relaxed completely.

I closed my eyes and tilted my head back against the ledge, enjoying it. But I wouldn't fall asleep here. There was too much to do, and I didn't know how long it would be before my father returned from his meetings. I resigned myself to getting out and left the warm water, drying myself off with a towel. The servants had set me fresh clothes.

It was a loose-fitting Grand Rislandian Army uniform, baggy around my sides, but it was the best they had in this situation. In hindsight, I should have brought a bag or suitcase with me from the airship. I still appreciated their kindness and dressed in the uniform.

After giving my thick hair a good brushing, I explored the insides of the castle. It was much smaller than King Malaky's palace, as to be expected, but it was still sizable enough to house a good number of our army's representatives.

For the first time, I also saw members of our navy. They were in similar uniform to mine, but in a dark blue color with silver buttons. Since obtaining my airship, I had spent most of my time flying over land. Our times over sea were in transit, and I hadn't come across the other branch of our military. Their function was more to protect our ports, and there weren't very many of them.

People didn't recognize me without my Baron von Monocle attire. It had a flair to it, and the red cape was a dead giveaway. Now, I looked like any other soldier. It was nice to be able to explore the halls and rooms without having people treat me like I were some hero. I still didn't feel like I had done anything to deserve such praise.

There were at least dozens of officers inside this castle, perhaps as many as two hundred. These had to be the best of the army to be able to be in my father's inner circle. The best outside of my crew, that was. I smiled to myself as I considered how wonderful my people were.

"Baron von Monocle," a man said.

I turned, recognizing Sergeant Lansing from Rislandia City. "Not so loud. I'm enjoying the anonymity," I said.

He saluted me. "Very well. Good to see you made it out."

"Likewise." I returned the salute. "How are you holding up here?"

"Being honest?" He shrugged. "This is the first time in my life it's felt like we weren't going to come out of everything alright. But the general says you have a new plan that might get us out of this? I'd heard stories of the old days, when he captained your airship. People say he came out of nowhere and saved the day, from Portsgate all the way to Borderville. Looks like you inherited his knack, hmm?"

I couldn't help but flush with embarrassment. "I wouldn't say that. I'm only doing what I can for Rislandia. Just like the rest of us."

"Well, it's appreciated. Spirits lifted quite a bit here just hearing the airship landed. I can't wait to get revenge on those Wyranth mutants."

"Mutants?" I laughed.

"That's what they are, right? Not entirely human since they started ingesting giant's blood. So the rumors go, at least."

"Well, hopefully we've put an end to any more of that, too."

My father turned a corner up ahead. He scanned the corridors looking for me but hadn't seen me yet. "It was good talking with you, Sergeant. Best of luck out there. I need to see my father," I said, pointing.

Sergeant Lansing looked back to my father. "No problem. Good luck to you, as well."

My father caught sight of me and stepped toward me with purpose. "There you are. I went to the tubs looking for you."

"I decided to explore a little."

He smiled. "That's my girl. Ready to see Talyen and your baby sister?"

"As I'll ever be." I smiled back at him.

He motioned and turned back the way he'd come from. "Follow me."

We made our way up winding spiral stairs to the second floor of the castle and over into one of the rooms. Talyen rested in a bed with several fluffy pillows behind her. She held a small little thing in her arms, which had no hair. A midwife hovered around her, pouring a glass of water and setting it on her nightstand.

"Hello," my father said in an almost sultry manner.

"Theo," Talyen said, looking up at us, her eyes bright with affection for my father. "And Zaira. A nice surprise. Come on in."

We both made our way to the foot of the bed.

"I'll leave you three alone," the midwife said, scurrying out of the room.

"How's the baby?" my father asked.

"Good," Talyen said. "Would you like to hold her?"

My father leaned over, and Talyen handed the baby to him. He cradled her in his arms like she was the most precious thing in the world. Her eyes were shut but it didn't stop him from making strange gurgling noises at her. People acted so strange around babies.

I watched my father interacting with Lilly. Seeing him so consumed with someone else didn't make me jealous. I was happy for him and Talyen, though I wished I could have had a relationship with him where he was home more often. Now it was me always away. One day, we'd be able to sit around a table and share a meal like a normal family.

"How is the airship?" Talyen asked.

I pried my attention away from the little baby to look at her. Talyen didn't have any makeup on and had dark circles under her eyes. Her hair was tangled and messy, and wrinkles covered her gown. I'd never seen her worn down before, and it was strange to see it now. Was having a child really that difficult?

The sight of her was so jarring it almost made me forget her question. "Oh," I said, recomposing myself. "Good. The crew is perfect, as you know. Sometimes, it feels like it'd run just as well without me."

"We both know that's not true," Talyen said.

I nodded, though I wasn't as sure it was the truth as she was. "But you know how it is. We found another one of those giant creatures, if you hadn't heard."

"I hadn't. I knew you had discovered the Wyranth had a new supply of their serum. Did you destroy it?"

"We did. Though we wanted to keep it under our control so we could produce an anti-serum. Which we did, but we only have enough to impact the Wyranth for one major battle."

"Let's hope it's enough."

My father looked up from Lilly. "It will be," he said. "Have a little faith. We've always managed before. I'd been meaning to talk to you about that, my love."

Talyen's eyes twinkled at him. "Hmm?"

"We're going to have to move out in the next couple of days. It's now or never," he said.

"I was afraid you'd say something like that. And I suppose you wish me to stay here with Lilly?"

"Of course. Because—"

She held up a finger to cut off his words. "If worst comes to worst, I can get on one of the ships and flee to Atrebla. I figured you would plan something like that. But you're the general now, don't forget. You don't need to go up on the front lines and play hero like you used to do."

"Well, I—"

Talyen glowered at him. "Seriously, Theo. You have a new baby."

I patted my father on the arm. "I've got this," I told him.

He looked between the two of us. "You've got me outnumbered."

"And outgunned," Talyen said.

My father sighed. "Okay. I promise I won't try anything foolish."

"Good. The last time you did you ended up in a Wyranth prison for two years. Don't forget it."

"I won't." He smiled sheepishly. "Oh," he said, holding Lilly toward me, "would you like to hold your baby sister, Zaira?"

The question caught me off guard, and I found myself stepping backward. "I... I haven't held a baby before."

"Don't worry about it," Talyen said. "It's odd for me, too, but once you have her in your arms, instinct will take over. You'll see."

They both stared at me expectantly. I wasn't going to get out of this. My father moved toward me. I carefully outstretched my arms. When he transferred Lilly's weight to me, I felt like I was going to drop the poor little thing, but she fell into my arms without a problem. She was much lighter than I envisioned her being, weighing almost nothing at all. And she was very warm. Her face looked so smooshed together, almost like a cartoon drawing of a person. But she was adorable in her own way.

I clutched her to my chest. My lip began to quiver. I loved her so much I wanted to cry. "She's wonderful," I said.

"Isn't she?" Talyen beamed.

After a while, I became comfortable holding Lilly, and I didn't want to let her go. My father took her back anyway. We talked a little about the plan, filling Talyen in on what we would be doing this next week and reminisced about old times. It was joyful being around my family, and I never wanted to leave. But the war had other plans, and I had to make sure my crew was ready.

We said our goodbyes, and my father ushered me back downstairs. "Do you want a place to stay in the castle?" he asked.

I shook my head. "I should get back to my ship." *My home,* I thought.

A tinge of sadness appeared in my father's eye. It was his ship as well. He missed it. But his place wasn't with the *Liliana* anymore. "Very well," he said, pulling me in to a tight embrace. "Say hello to Harkerpal for me."

"I will," I said and turned to depart the castle.

CHAPTER 24

I met with King Malaky and his son, who's nearer to my age. They have a plan to bring yet more knights to the border, in hopes of removing the Wyranth's leadership. If we can do that, they will be in disarray.

An excerpt From Baron von Monocle's Log
Day 12 of the Month of the Fool
24th Year of King Malaky XV's Reign

PREPARING FOR A heavy battle isn't the funnest of jobs for an airship captain. The crew had so many supply orders to fill, so many items needing repair, and I had to try to coax everything I could out of the army's supply masters. From oil to grease for the turbines to new uniforms to replace some of the crew's torn ones, there was a list over a hundred pages long. With little time to spare, I had to sift through and try to obtain the most important of the items. We wouldn't get everything we wanted, even if the fate of Rislandia rested on our anti-serum scheme.

The deckhands ran drills from dawn until dusk, working on combat tactics both aerial and groundside, as well as doing speed drills to facilitate emergency evacuations. I walked back and forth on the deck while these went on, trying to look serious and as if I were watching them diligently. The truth was, I trusted them to do their jobs far more than I trusted myself to correct them if they were making any errors.

First Sergeant Wright was not as forgiving as I was. He shouted at several of the crew, getting so close to their faces he probably spat on them while he was yelling. I was glad I didn't come up through the enlisted ranks.

Down below, the cannoneers ran similar drills. Marina took charge of the below decks action. I crossed through there and checked on Harkerpal and his team. They were putting the finishing touches on the anti-serum sprayer, which took the form of a tapped line protruding from the large barrel crate that held the liquid. The line had an automatic crank, powered by a small steam motor. Out the other side was an exhaust, which extended through the side of the hull.

"You've produced all the anti-serum you can? And how does this work?" I asked.

Rhys nodded. "Ready to go. I'll let my friend here tell you about the crop dusting mechanism." He motioned to Harkerpal.

"It will be fully automatic. All we have to do is flip this lever," Harkerpal pointed to a small handle on the side of one of the pipes, "and the motor will push the liquid through the line. The speed is key because it will disperse evenly through a small grate at the end, which we can't see from here."

"I'm incredibly impressed with your engineer's design abilities," Rhys said. "When this is over, we might make a good team to create some modern inventions and change the way of life for many Rislandians."

"I look forward to it," Harkerpal said, lifting his chin proudly.

I clasped my hands together. "I'm glad it's ready. Who will be down here to manage it?"

"I will," Rhys said.

Harkerpal bobbed his head. "Just call through the communications funnel and he should be able to hear you. Simple enough."

It sounded simple, but I still didn't feel great about the whole plan. Now that we were getting close, jitters were getting to me.

What if we missed? What if the serum was ineffective in this form? There were so many variables we didn't have time to test.

But my father told me I had to have faith. He was right. I let out a deep breath.

Rhys shuffled to the side, checking the components of the device.

Harkerpal stood watching me. "You know, the first time your father ushered the *Liliana* into battle, he was nervous like you are today. You both take the edge of your cape, right by your pocket and rub it between your thumb and middle finger. It's how I can tell," he said, pointing to me.

I realized I was doing exactly as he said and stopped, letting my hand fall by my side.

Harkerpal laughed. "It's nothing to be embarrassed about. We're all on edge. The crew is as nervous as you are, you have to remember. They look to you for comfort."

I frowned, not sure what he'd meant. "What should I do?"

"Do you know what gets the crew excited more than almost anything?" He said, tilting his head at me with amusement in his eyes.

"What's that?" I asked. I bit my lip, figuring I should know the answer to this better than I did. But Harkerpal didn't look on me with any judgment.

"Promotions."

I laughed this time. "Do you want a promotion? You've done more than your fair share. I don't know exactly what to promote you *to* from chief engineer, though."

"No, no. Not for me. For someone else. Find someone deserving and call the crew in. It'll be a joyous affair and will ease everyone's spirits."

I'd never considered promoting people before. Was it even something I was allowed to do? My place within the Grand Rislandian Army was fuzzy, undefined. Everyone seemed to respect my authority, but I didn't want to step on any of the real military officers' toes. "I'm not even sure who to promote," I said.

Harkerpal smiled. "You'll think of someone. Don't worry about it too much, though, it's just an idea." He shrugged.

"Thanks, Harkerpal. I'll leave you to this then." I gave him a firm nod and departed the room, heading back into the main cargo bay where the ramp was still open to the outside world. I walked, intending on going back to the bridge, lost in thought. Who would I promote? There were so many people. First Sergeant Wright came to mind. He did such a good job. Or perhaps one of his commandos? I would have to ask him who would be best in that instance. I really wanted to promote everyone. It didn't seem fair to single one person out.

"I know that look," a male voice said.

Not expecting anyone to be there, I tensed and froze. It took me a moment to recompose myself. Ethan von Lantern stood on the ramp, arms crossed over his chest.

He smiled, dropped his arms, and made his way up the ramp. "Did I startle you?"

I ran a hand back through my hair. "I was a little lost in thought."

"What about?" He stopped right next to me.

"Ah, airship command stuff." I don't know why I was so coy with the talk of promotions. It still didn't feel like I should be the one making the decisions, let alone talking about them with one of the knights.

"Fair enough. I actually needed to talk to you about airship matters," he said. His fingers brushed against mine.

The touch stilled my breath. It sent my head swimming every time he came near me lately. Even though it was cool outside, I felt like I was burning up. "Oh?" I managed to say.

He nodded, the smile falling from his face. "When you look at me like that..." He turned his head to the side. "No, now's not the time. The knights need me for the assault. I'm going to be going with the ground units and won't be able to come with you and the airship."

My heart sank. I'd never considered Ethan leaving me. He'd become such an important part of the crew I'd forgotten he had obligations elsewhere. This meant he'd be running directly into danger. He might even get killed. I didn't want that at all. "There's no way you can stay?" I pleaded.

Ethan shook his head. "It's not up to me. Trust me, I want to be here with you... with the *Liliana*."

It was all I wanted, as well. I felt my lips twisting into a frown by instinct, but I tried to keep my face expressionless. If someone came by and saw us, I didn't want them to see me shaken. "So, you came to say goodbye."

He turned back to me. His eyes were moist, shining. He wouldn't break down and cry, but he felt just as strongly as I did. Seeing the intense emotion from him brought me comfort for some strange reason. "Yeah." His voice was low, soft.

I wanted to melt into his arms. I found myself standing on the tips of my toes, thirsty for his kiss.

He brought his lips to mine. We touched. His arms slipped around me. I parted my lips, and in a shocking sensation, felt his tongue. It was odd at first, but I found I liked it. It was warm. He didn't try to overwhelm me, just teased me with the extra touch. We kissed for several long moments before I pulled back.

"If someone saw us," I said, nervously gripping my cape. Harkerpal had been right about my habits. I'd never noticed them.

"Who cares," Ethan said.

"I do!"

"It's not like they don't know we have a... thing going. What is this anyway?"

I shook my head. "I don't know. And I don't think I have the time to figure it out right now."

"You're right." Ethan cast his eyes downward. "Anyway, I just wanted you to know, you know, how I felt. I know we kissed before, but I don't even know how to say this."

"I think you're saying it just fine," I said. My heart beat so hard I wanted to tell it to shush. "I feel the same way."

He looked up again. "You do?"

I nodded.

Ethan clenched a fist with determination. "Great. I mean... not great we have to go off into war. Timing, yeah?"

"Yeah."

"Anyway, you stay safe up there. I want to see you again when this is over."

"I was about to say the same thing to you." I forced a smile.

Our eyes met one more time, and we stood in silence, gazing at each other for far too long. Neither of us wanted to leave. I didn't want to think about the implications that I might never see him again. This was the last thing we should have been discussing right now! There was too much to do before we set off to war in earnest. Why did life get in the way at the most inconvenient times?

"Okay then. Good—"

"Don't say that," I said, holding up a finger to quiet him. "It sounds so final. I don't want to think about that. Okay?"

"Okay," Ethan said, letting out a deep breath. "I don't know why this is so hard."

"Me either. It's something we'll have to figure out after the battle, yeah?"

"You're right. Good luck, Baron von Monocle!" Ethan said and turned to descend the ramp.

"Good luck, Ethan von Lantern," I said quietly to myself after he was out of earshot.

My mind whirled. I couldn't think straight at all. How was I supposed to come up with someone to promote when Ethan's eyes cluttered my mind? His face. The shape of his chin. His firm arms. His warm lips. All I wanted to do was run after him and tell him he didn't have to leave just then. But he did. Whatever the knights were planning would require even more intensive training than we had on the airship.

I resolved to push Ethan from my mind as I proceeded to the stairs. I had to get myself focused. What was I going to do? The crew was counting on me to provide some sort of moral support.

Without coming any closer to a conclusion on what I would say, who I would promote, or what I needed to do, I found myself on the *Liliana's* top deck once more. Most of the crew were assembled there, finishing up a training session and resting. They talked amongst themselves, drank water, and relaxed. Some had towels, wiping sweat off their brows. Whatever drill First Sergeant Wright had put them through must have been taxing.

I made my way to the aft turbine and stepped onto the small platform surrounding it. I could see everyone a little more clearly, and the mere act of moving like that made the crew turn and face me. This was the time to speak, that much was certain. But what would I say? Didn't promotions require more pomp and ceremony than a simple declaration?

The crew's eyes were expectant, so I cleared my throat. I would have to wing it. "Soon, we will be setting upon one of the most important battles in Rislandia's history," I said, a nervous lump forming in my throat. I'd given speeches before, but I had always been more confident in our missions. We couldn't be assured victory this time. "I believe in all of you. You are the best our country has to offer, and we'll show the Wyranth what it means to be Rislandian."

Those words brought forth a couple of whistles from the crowd.

I raised my chin. "While we're on the topic, some of you have shown exemplary skill at your posts. I want to highlight... a few of you in that regard." As I spoke, more people stepped forward. I scanned some of the familiar faces. I would have to make my decisions quickly. My eyes fell upon Wright. He would be a good choice. "First Sergeant," I said.

"Yes, Captain?" Wright said, stepping forward.

"You've excelled in your duties beyond what I could have ever anticipated. For that, I wish to show you my gratitude, and the gratitude of this crew."

Several people started clapping, but I held a hand up to let them know I wasn't finished speaking. They quieted.

"Therefore, by, uh…" I had to think of something to say. "…the power vested in me by King Malaky, I hereby promote you to Sergeant Major."

Just as Harkerpal had anticipated, the surprise promotion caused the crew to erupt in cheers. Everyone clapped. Several of the men slapped Wright on the back.

"But that's not all," I said. I glanced toward the bridge. Major Ral and Lieutenant Colwell stood there, behind the crowd toward the back. The last people who ever received recognition because they were almost always behind the command consoles. "Ral, Colwell, come here!"

The crew laughed. They clapped rhythmically, adding to the drama of the moment as my two bridge officers came forward.

"Major Ral, you've held an enlisted ground soldier's rank long enough. That changes today. I hereby declare you to be promoted to the officer rank of Lieutenant. Lieutenant Colwell, you've run this airship like clockwork. I'm forever indebted to you, and I wish I could do more for you. But for now, you will hereby be Lieutenant Commander," I said.

The crew clapped and cheered. Someone among the deckhands shouted, "Hip hip!" Which was then followed by "Hooray!" by the crew. They repeated the cheer two more times.

Everyone seemed to be so joyful. It made me swell with pride. I wanted to promote each and every member of the crew, but then it wouldn't have the impact as the symbolic ones I'd chosen. I clasped my hands together. "It's well-earned. You three have been invaluable to me. I'm not sure I'd even be alive today if it weren't for you."

Several of the crew chuckled.

"It's our privilege," Commander Colwell said.

"It's a privilege for all of us to be on the *Liliana*," I said. "For me as well. And I know when we go out into this battle, it won't be our last. We will fend off the Wyranth and push them back. We will retake our great city and see the beautiful Crystal Spire on our horizon once more. We need to give it our all, and I know each and every one of you will do just that. King Malaky is depending on us." I pointed over the side of the ship toward the castle. "The people are depending on us. We will not fail them."

"No, we won't!" several of the crew echoed.

"For now, relax, enjoy yourselves, celebrate the promotion of your peers. Tomorrow, we fight. For steam and country!"

"For steam and country!" the entire crew shouted louder than I'd ever heard them before. It was loud enough to rattle the hull of the airship and carry down to the castle beyond.

CHAPTER 25

The deck is full of knights. Our engines held the strain of the extra weight without issue. Let's hope this works.

An excerpt From Baron von Monocle's Log
Day 13 of the Month of the Fool
24th Year of King Malaky XV's Reign

THE CREW DIDN'T celebrate their last evening before battle nearly as much as I would have expected. Everyone turned in early after congratulating the newly-promoted crewmen. The danger loomed too real to have too much merriment. I found myself unable to sleep and, instead, poured over my father's logs, trying to find some wisdom. So many people comment on "the luck of the von Monocles" that there had to be some advice I could glean from his adventures.

I found his logs to be very basic, simple descriptions of what had occurred. They were more statements of history than of tactics. His personal worries were apparent, especially about losing me or my mother, but I didn't see anything that would help us for the next day's important battle. He might have designed his log this way intentionally. If the Wyranth captured his words, they could use them against us.

After skimming through the pages, it appeared as if he really did will his way into victory more times than not. Did life work that way? Was confidence the difference between a poor and great leader? I couldn't believe willpower could be the only factor, but I resolved to be less hard on myself about my command abilities.

I'd already grown in that regard. Thinking back to when I'd first inherited my airship, I'd had no faith in myself. I'd even crashed the ship on my first time flying. It was amazing how a few months of working could change a person. And change my crew. They didn't doubt my orders or me. I finally belonged here. I wasn't faking it anymore.

The words on the pages blurred. I hadn't actually been reading them in some time but reflecting on my life. Was this what people did when they worried about death? I didn't want to die. I had so much to do. But this was the life I chose. If I hadn't, I would be one of those poor people huddled in the streets, helpless to do anything to defend themselves against this ever-advancing menace. That could never be me.

I closed the logbook and flopped onto my bed. Toby immediately hopped onto my stomach and began nuzzling me playfully. I petted him, and he gnawed on my fingers. The ferret was uncanny. He knew me well enough to sense my moods, to know when I needed comfort. Or at least it seemed like he did. "I love you so much, Toby," I said, giving him a squeeze.

Toby squawked.

"You fought these battles, too. Don't think I forgot your escape from here. We'll have none of that this time, you hear me?"

He crawled onto my chest and sniffed at my chin, his wet nose tickling me.

I sighed. Too many worries spun through my head. So many things could go wrong in the next day's battle. Worse, I didn't know what the knights and Ethan would be doing. They would probably be in the most danger of anyone. I didn't want to think about it at all. Why couldn't I stop my thoughts? I needed to rest.

"Alright, Toby," I said, lifting him and setting him to the side. "I need to try to sleep."

I closed my eyes. It took a long time for sleep to come, and when someone woke me up by knocking on my door, I felt like I hadn't rested at all.

The sun peeked through the portal at the back of my quarters. It was light. It meant we would have to lift off soon. The crew knew I liked to sleep in as late as possible. My head was fuzzy from being so tired, but I wouldn't let it slow me down. I had a job to do.

I rushed out of bed and quickly dressed myself. More knocks came to the door. "Coming, coming!" I said.

I opened the door to find Marina there. "Wake up call," she said.

"Time to get this ship flying," I said. "And thanks."

"No problem. You nervous?" Marina asked.

"Yeah. How could I not be? Barely got any sleep."

"You'll do fine. I just wish we had more cannonballs. I wanted to talk to you before we left to let you know we're on low supply. We'll probably only be able to get a couple of volleys in," Marina said.

I stepped out of my room and shut the door behind me. "That's okay. We won't be relying on cannonballs if all goes well."

Marina nodded. "An interesting plan. Rhys is rather innovative. It's fun to watch him work with Harkerpal, who can execute his visions with ease. I think he's enjoying being here."

"Good." I grinned. "We're lucky he had an eye for one of our cannoneers. I'd best get up there."

"Good luck, Baronette!" Marina said.

I found my way to the stairs and stepped out onto the deck. The crew were at their stations, ready. Several of the deckhands saluted me as I passed. This would be the moment of truth. The weight of the mission knotted my shoulders as tense as they'd ever been. Nervousness made my stomach grumble.

In theory, I should have headed to the mess to eat something before taking my place on the bridge. But I didn't feel hungry exactly. I'm not sure I could have stomached food. Even so, I kept my face as impassive as possible. The crew didn't need to know how nervous I was.

When I arrived at the bridge, Commander Colwell and Lieutenant Ral saluted me. They both had their new rank pips pinned to their uniforms, and the twinkles in both men's eyes let me know they were proud to have them.

I saluted in return. "Are we ready to go?" I asked.

"We can take off on your word, ma'am," Lieutenant Ral said.

"Let's do it," I said.

Ral turned the ignition. The engine *whirred,* noise rattling the deck. The blades turned on the giant turbines, gaining speed with each rotation. The ship was so complex, operating with such beauty in its design, I'd never truly taken the time to appreciate it. I was glad to do so now. It might be the last time I ever saw the ship start up.

We lifted into the air. Cliffside Castle faded beneath us, becoming smaller, and then nothing but a speck in our field of vision. People in the streets cheered as we took off, a roar of a giant crowd gathered below.

"I won't let you down," I said quietly.

"What's that?" Commander Colwell asked.

"Talking to myself," I said.

We didn't converse further as the turbines shifted, moving the ship southward toward Rislandia City. We had to time our launch carefully so as not to give away our precise troop locations. The infantry had gone ahead of us, the airship able to cover distances much faster than they could on foot. They would be waiting to see us in the sky to begin their assault, in hopes the airship could provide at least a small distraction before we began our true task.

The Wyranth would never know what hit them.

That was the hope, at least.

We sailed across the countryside. The journey only lasted a few minutes until we saw the lines of our Rislandian troops on the horizon. The Wyranth wouldn't be too much farther ahead.

Colwell had his eye pressed to the telescope, getting a better view of the groundside situation. "Oh no," he said.

"What's that?"

"The troops have already engaged the enemy. It looks like we're late."

"It can't be," Lieutenant Ral said. He produced a pocket watch and frowned, looking at its face. "We were precisely on time."

"The Wyranth must have known our people were coming. They advanced on our lines. There are already a lot of casualties," Colwell said.

"Then we can't spare any time. Let's get there faster," I said.

Ral pushed the controls to increase the ship's velocity. The ground became a blur beneath us. It wasn't long before we flew over the center of the conflict.

A flare went up from the infantry below. Our ship was moving so fast to try to engage with the Wyranth lines, could we stop to answer it?

"Lieutenant Ral, can you bring us about?" I asked.

"Aye," he said, maneuvering the controls to bank our ship around toward the flare.

"Send down a rope ladder. Whoever's down there wants to tell us something important or they wouldn't have put a flare up," I said.

"On it," Colwell said, hustling out to the deck to relay my orders. The deckhands quickly unwound one of the ropes and dropped it below.

With precision, Ral brought the Liliana to a halt where the smoke still loomed in the air. No one could fly this ship like him.

I made my way out to the deck, my cape flowing behind me. The deckhands pulled the rope up quickly, bringing an infantryman aboard. He looked like he'd seen a lot of battle already, his gray uniform scratched and worn, his face blackened with dirt.

He saluted me.

"Name and rank?" Colwell asked.

"Private Forster Hudson, sir."

"At ease," I said. "What's going on down below?"

Private Hudson let out a deep breath. "I was part of the scouting party that went ahead. Our men are holding our own despite the Wyranth advancing faster than we anticipated. The problem is, they're acting even more aggressive than usual. It's hard to explain, but they're ferocious. It's causing some morale problems," he said.

"The giant's blood. We saw that before. We need to get the anti-serum delivered quickly," I said.

"It's more than that, ma'am," Private Hudson said. He rubbed his hands together nervously. "Like I said, I was scouting. I'm the only one from my unit to make it back to the front. There's something in the Old Forest. I couldn't get farther. The Wyranth slaughtered the rest of the scouts. But whatever it is, I think it's driving the Wyranth insane with rage."

"Another giant exerting its will?" Colwell asked, raising a brow at me.

"It might be." I bit my lower lip. Could we have missed another one? Buried somewhere in the forest? It would make for another hiding place where we wouldn't have easily found one.

I considered the prospect. The giants caused the earthquakes, at least they seemed to. We'd felt quakes under the Wyranth capital, where we found a giant. We felt one in Plainsroad Village, and subsequently found a giant in the mine. But Rislandia City wasn't close to either of those places. It would make sense for there to be a third giant nearby. With all the commotion, we hadn't had time to rationally think all of this through. We'd missed one. And the Wyranth still had their supply of the serum despite all of our efforts.

"Thank you for bringing this information, soldier," I said, turning. I motioned to Colwell to follow me back to the bridge. "We'll take this into consideration. Escort Private Hudson to Dr. du Clockhand and make sure he gets any medical attention he needs," I said to the deckhands.

"Aye, ma'am," one of the men said. They took the infantryman away.

I hurried toward the bridge, Colwell keeping pace at my side.

"What do we do with this information? Do we head for the forest?" Colwell asked.

"Not yet," I said. "I think we give our infantry some relief first, proceed with the plan. Then we head toward the forest."

Colwell nodded. We stepped back to the bridge.

"Are you ready, Lieutenant Ral?" I asked. "You're going to have to fly like you've never flown before."

"I am," Ral said, keeping his hands on the controls.

"Then let's go. Break for the Wyranth soldiers and we'll implement the plan."

Colwell and I stood at the ready, watching while Ral turned the ship back toward the advancing enemy force. We still flew high enough in the air that the soldiers below only looked like little specks. Colwell manned the telescope, but I could imagine the fierce battles down below. The gunshots. The wounds. The death. I'd seen enough of it in my time. I only hoped our people were holding on. "How are they doing?" I mustered the courage to ask.

"The line doesn't appear to be moving one way or another. Both side are reinforcing their front lines very well. There will be a lot of casualties today," Colwell said.

I let out a deep breath. So many friends, so many loved ones. Ethan. I couldn't think about him right now. I had to have faith he would be okay.

The ship continued forward, and we dropped in altitude. Ral maneuvered us quickly so we wouldn't be an easy target for the Wyranth. We rushed toward the earth below. As the Wyranth came into view, it was clear just how large the scope of this battle was. There were thousands of them. I'd never seen anything like it before on any of my prior missions. Surface cannons fired.

A *boom* sounded just off our starboard bow.

"Careful," I said, as if it would do any good. Ral had to focus as much on his diving run as he could. If the Wyranth managed to hit us, there was nothing we could do.

We were mere feet off the ground when Ral brought us level with the earth. We zoomed toward the Wyranth soldiers, probably frightening several of ours on the front line in the process. I leaned into the communications funnel. "Rhys! Spray the anti-serum!"

Colwell still had his eye through the telescope. "It's working. I see the spray. It's a dark blue cloud, looks almost like dust," he said.

"Probably why they call it crop dusting," I said. It sounded more patronizing than I would have liked, but I meant the words to be serious.

The force of the forward motion weighed on me, and I gripped onto the hand rail. Lieutenant Ral maneuvered us expertly, giving us enough time to spray a large amount of the anti-serum over the Wyranth forces.

Looking through the side windows, I saw the spray coming from the back of the ship. It was a wide distribution, able to cover a lot of the soldiers. We would need a few more runs to make a dent in their forces, but we also had to be careful not to hit any of our own soldiers and pacify them.

We reached the back of the Wyranth forces, and Ral banked us to the side. My window tilted toward the ground below. Several Wyranth soldiers had their weapons pointed toward us, and we were still low enough that I could see them clearly. They fired their rifles, and for once, they had an opportunity to hit us in the airship. My eyes went wide.

I ducked.

The glass of the window shattered above me. I covered my neck with my hands as the shards fell onto me. The cuts stung, and I let out a small yelp.

"Baronette!" Colwell shouted, heading over to me. He crouched by my side and touched my arm.

"I'm fine. We need to tell Rhys to stop spraying the serum until we make our next run," I said. I bled in several places on my hands, and glass shards littered my hair.

Colwell moved without hesitation. He spoke into the communications funnel. The wind roared outside as we moved at incredible speeds. I stood and let the glass fall down the back of me. It didn't feel like any made its way into my blouse, thankfully. I looked at the back of my hands and saw a few cuts, one of them fairly deep. They hurt, but they wouldn't incapacitate me.

Above me, a bullet was lodged into the wooden wall of the bridge. Based on where it came from, it would have been exactly where my head had been a moment prior. The luck of the von Monocles again? Or maybe we just had the good sense to know when to duck.

I shook my head a couple of times to get as many more shards out as I could, and then moved back to the safety rail. I wouldn't stand right by the window again, not this close to the ground.

Ral completed our loop around, and we flew back over our Rislandian troops, heading for the Wyranth. "Get ready," I said. We sped forward and reached the front battle line once more. "Now!"

"Deploy anti-serum," Colwell said through the funnel.

This time, I didn't look to see if Rhys complied. He would. This was all working according to plan. Hope grew within me for the first time in days. The jitters had all but disappeared. If the worst the Wyranth could do was to shatter some glass on my head, then the *Liliana* could make the difference in this war.

"Almost there," Colwell said, staring through the telescope.

"We've got this," I said, more to myself than the other two on the bridge.

Then, something exploded, rocking the *Liliana* like I'd never felt before.

CHAPTER 26

We've dropped the knights behind enemy lines. It's up to them now. We'll be regrouping with our forces and readying for battle.

An excerpt From Baron von Monocle's Log
Day 15 of the Month of the Fool
24th Year of King Malaky XV's Reign

THE SHIP TIPPED to its side. I barely managed to grab onto the hand rail to hold on for dear life. Commander Colwell wasn't so lucky. Having been hunched over the telescope a moment prior, he went flying to the side. His neck jerked back, and he hit his head hard against the wall. Lieutenant Ral braced himself, his feet wedged against the controls and the other side wall. He frantically adjusted the controls to try to right the *Liliana* again.

"She's not flying right," Ral said. He pulled down on one of the levers, hard.

It was all I could do to just hold on. Ral was the only one who could save us now. I snuck a glance toward Colwell. He lay slumped on the ground. Was he dead?

Ral managed to get the ship level again somehow. Another explosion sounded near us. "They've got their artillery turned on us now," he said. "I knew we were flying too close for too long."

Did we have a bad tactical plan? We had no choice. We had to try to manipulate the Wyranth soldiers with our anti-serum. The ship flew past the bulk of the army, the airship lifting further into the sky. I took a moment to move to Colwell's side. I touched him lightly. A few moments prior, he had been concerned for me, and all I had to show for it was a few cuts. But hitting his head that hard, he could be dead. Was he?

I couldn't tell. I put my hand in front of his face.

A soft, warm breath tickled my palm. He lived. There would be nothing I could do for him now. He needed the medic, but it was likely he wouldn't be the only one injured from the blast.

A young man stepped onto the bridge, saluting before his face turned ghost white. "Ah... sirs?" It was an innocent face, the man who first guarded me when I had to be confined to quarters on the ship, Ensign Glen Matthews.

I straightened and returned the salute. "Ensign Matthews, report."

His eyes darted over to Commander Colwell, crumpled on the floor. "Ah," he mumbled again, before shaking his head. "Sorry. I wasn't expecting to see... you know." He jutted his thumb behind him. "You should really come below decks, Baronette. The damage is severe. The Wyranth blew a hole clear through the back of the ship."

My stomach sank. "Rhys?"

"Oh! Sorry. He's alive. Shaken up from the blast, but he'll survive."

That was a relief. I didn't know what I'd do if we lost Rhys now. He had done so much for us and meant so much to Marina. It wasn't something I could stop and think about. "Okay, I'll head below decks, as long as you've got everything under control, Lieutenant Ral?"

"I'm doing the best I can. She's wobbly, but I think I can steer her true as long as we don't get hit again."

"Ensign Matthews. Find Dr. du Clockhand and make sure she attends to Commander Colwell. Lieutenant Ral, make sure he doesn't fall or bump his head any further while we're waiting for the doctor."

"Aye, ma'am," Ral said.

Matthews nodded.

I glanced out the side to see we were lifting up into white clouds. The Wyranth would hardly be able to target us here while we were in the middle of the battle. I wanted to look down and see if the serum took effect, but Ensign Matthews' expression told me I couldn't delay in seeing what had happened below. "You have the bridge then," I said, and followed Matthews out the door.

We hurried across the deck to the mess and then made our way down the stairs. Matthews veered off to the middle deck where the quarters and medical bay were located, and I descended to the bottom of the ship. I looped around until I came to the back compartment and stopped at the entrance.

The whole rear starboard section of the ship had become one gaping hole, with char marks having burnt through splinters of wood all around it. It was a large enough a hole to have four people able to stand in it and still not be able to fill it. Before I could look out further and see what was going on in the battle below, Marina waved to me to get my attention.

She was seated beside Rhys on the opposite side of the room, safe against the wooden wall. Or at least we would have thought it was safe prior to this incident. "Marina! Rhys!" I said, moving carefully over to them. I didn't want to get near the big hole, especially with the way the ship had been turning and making me lose my balance as of late.

Rhys looked very worn. Sweat dripped down his face, and he let out a deep breath. "Even with seeing all the violence of the Nightmen city, I've never quite been so scared in my entire life," he said.

"I bet," I said. "How close did it come?"

He didn't reply. I glanced to Marina. Was he okay?

"His ears are probably still ringing. I think the blast did some damage. Might not hear well for a while... if ever," she said, sounding concerned.

"I'm sorry, did you say something?" Rhys asked, looking at Marina. He brought a hand to one of his ears and rubbed it, as if it would do any good.

"No, I'm sorry," I said, frowning. I hated war. What it took from people. All things considered, Rhys was lucky. I crossed my arms and surveyed the room. It appeared as if most of the anti-serum crop dusting device had been blown out with the wall. The Wyranth had scored a perfect hit.

"Rhys said he'd gotten about eighty percent of the anti-serum sprayed. We could have done one more pass, but we accomplished most of what we were going to do anyway," Marina said, preempting my question. She understood me so well, it was always nice to have her around.

"That's good," I said, "but did it work?"

"Only one way to see for sure, yeah?"

With a deep breath, I cautiously stepped toward the hole. I didn't dare get too close, but I wanted to be able to look out. Even getting close was disorienting, which was strange, since I was used to looking over the railings of the ship. Having no safety rail, it didn't feel natural, and I certainly didn't want to plummet to my doom. A little fluffy cloud passed beneath us, and I could see the ground clearly.

The armies looked like little ants struggling. But they moved haphazardly, spreading out in all directions. They were fleeing. My heart nearly leapt through my chest. "We did it. They're on the run," I said.

But as the view became clearer, I could see something was amiss. They were running in *all* directions. It meant our people were fleeing, too.

Something was making its way through the troops, which seemed to be coming from the Old Forest beyond. I couldn't get a good look at it, but it pulsed with a strange blue light. Something I'd seen before. Did the Wyranth create a new vehicle or some sort of mechanical construct out of the giant's blood?

"This isn't good, Baronette," Marina said.

I glanced at her. She had a spyglass up to her eye, aiming it toward the hole while she held Rhys with her other arm. "More of our people are running than theirs."

"Why? What is that thing?"

"I'm trying to get in focus," Marina said, twisting the glass, using her cheek to prop it up as she brought it into focus. Her jaw dropped. "You're not going to believe this."

"What?"

"It's one of those creatures. It's rampaging through the soldiers—Wyranth and Rislandian. One of those giants is on the move!"

I could hardly conceive what Marina was saying. I thought back to the tales of giants my father used to tell me as a child, trying to reconcile them with what I'd seen myself in the caves behind the Wyranth capital and in the mine near Plainsroad Village. I hadn't seen a cohesive creature, but a glowing blob, pulsing as it breathed. How had the story gone? I tried to remember the details.

A giant by the name of Golgmarsh wanted to touch the tip of the sky and climbed to the highest peak of the tallest mountain. The ground beneath him couldn't support his weight, so he fell off the mountain and thudded to the ground below. The resulting shake and thunderous boom cracked the world. Water spewed from beneath the ground, which created the Golgmarsh Ocean that lined the coast of Rislandia.

The old children's tale had roots in reality, as many old children's tales must have. My father confirmed a story, stating how the giants had a civilization of their own until their technology exploded, spewing chemicals across their land. They slowly transformed into the bulbous creatures I'd seen with my own eyes. They could project thoughts and feelings, sway battles, change the course of nations.

It all suddenly clicked for me. The Wyranth's "Project Walking Monster" had nothing to do with their armies marching. It hadn't been a code at all. Their scientists had been working on a way to get the giants mobile and use them as weapons!

This war was beyond one of simple armies clashing together. It was one of advancing technology. First, we had our airships, then they had their serums. While our scientists worked on a cure, theirs worked on creating more havoc within our lands. And they were succeeding. The giant creature down below plowed through soldiers as yet more ran.

Surely they knew they wouldn't be able to control such a monstrosity? Loosing such a creature on the world was too dangerous a proposition. I remembered having one of those things controlling my mind. It was an experience I never wanted to repeat. The helplessness...

My theories didn't matter now. The Wyranth did what they had done, all part of the Iron Emperor's plans. Whether he understood the danger or not didn't matter. What mattered was how Rislandia lay within this creature's path of destruction. Our soldiers were down there, and they wouldn't all be able to outrun that thing.

"I have to get back to the bridge," I said to Marina.

"I know," she said.

"I'm going to need you manning the cannons. We have to take that thing out," I said.

Rhys furrowed his brow. "I'm trying to read your lips but it's difficult. I see the creature down below. This is bad. Very bad." He pointed toward where the crop dusting device had been. The conveyor that drew the pump from the barrels of the anti-serum was mangled, the tube itself shattered. But the container was still there. "You might want to use this. We don't have all that much left, but it should act as a counter agent against that thing."

"Great idea," I said, trying to speak slowly so he could read my words better as I said them. "But how are we going to deploy it? Dump the barrel?"

"We can coat our remaining cannonballs in the liquid, and *then* dump the rest of the barrel," Marina said, grinning.

"I like this plan. Who knows if it'll work, but the anti-serum is meant to counteract the blood of those things, right? So, it's better than nothing. Marina, gather up the cannoneers. I'm going to return to the bridge so we can take this thing down without any further damage." I clasped my hands together. "Our work is never done, is it?"

"Not until every last Wyranth is out of this country," Marina said.

I nodded. "Let's go."

CHAPTER 27

The battle began in earnest today. It's one of the fiercest between our two peoples yet. I hope the knights succeed.

An excerpt From Baron von Monocle's Log
Day 20 of the Month of the Fool
24th Year of King Malaky XV's Reign

THE *LILIANA* CIRCLED around the monstrosity several times. I watched the creature through the periscope. Skin like jelly, pulsing with blue light, it was little different from the giant blobs we'd seen already, except this one had arms and legs. They weren't fully formed, no toes or fingers I could see. It reached out with long arms as if they were bludgeons and swiped at soldiers. Bullets didn't seem to have any effect on the creature. No matter how our people fought, it kept advancing. Standard weapons were useless.

It would be up to us.

Ensign Matthews returned to the bridge, saluting the three of us. "Sirs, the cannoneers report they are ready," he said.

"Thank you, Ensign. Return to your battle station," Commander Colwell said. He had a bandage around his skull, but he seemed like he was able to manage himself. Dr. du Clockhand had already left the bridge by the time I'd arrived. Whatever she'd done to get Colwell back on his feet, she had my gratitude.

When Matthews departed, I glanced to Lieutenant Ral. He had an unease on his face I'd never seen before. Usually so confident, his lips were now tight, nearly in a frown. He focused his eyes forward, hands on the controls, ever vigilant.

"Are you ready?" I asked.

"I'll do the best I can. Turning the ship with a big hole in the bottom of the hull isn't easy. Everything's off balance," Ral said.

"Just do your best. It's all we can ask." I turned to Colwell. "How about you?"

"Dr. du Clockhand's smelling salts gave me a start. She gave me a little something for the pain and wrapped my head. I'm not sure I need it, but she insisted. I'll be alright."

"Good," I said. "Let's get ready then."

The ship banked downward. It shook as it moved, not nearly as stable as it used to be before we had our gaping hole. But we still managed to slope downward in a spiral around the giant. It came into view on the starboard side and stayed in view. The creature noticed us and flung its arms in the direction of the airship. Its effort proved futile. Even though it stood more than twenty feet tall, we would always be able to go higher.

The distraction allowed a few of our soldiers to get further away from it. They'd avoid the creature's next swings as well as our volley of cannonballs.

"Fire now!" I shouted, forgetting only the bridge crew could hear me.

Colwell leaned into the communications funnel. "Starboard cannoneers, fire all weapons."

The familiar *boom* resounded as the cannons erupted simultaneously. This time it followed with a *crack*.

"That can't be good," I said. Colwell and I both froze, looking at each other. It had to be the hull, already stressed from being hit before. But we had to rely on the old ship to hold together.

I turned quickly to see if the giant had been hit. The creature seemed to absorb the cannonballs at first, but then it writhed and made an ear-piercing, screeching sound. It resonated so loudly even this high in the air, I could only imagine how terrible it must have been on the ground. I covered my ears.

"We did it," I said.

"Not so fast," Colwell said, pointing.

The giant shook, and then resumed its path of terror, slashing its arms wildly at soldiers. Several of our men took devastating blows even as they tried to run away. The giant seemed even angrier than before.

The *Liliana* turned about, wobbling in the air as Ral tried to keep her stable. The port side now faced the giant, but it wasn't going to stay still for us this time. It followed our soldiers north, moving at an incredible pace. Our airship was still much faster. We ran the creature down.

This time, I leaned into the funnel. "Port cannoneers, fire!" I shouted.

The cannons blasted, jolting the ship once more. The turbines sputtered, causing a moment of turbulence before the ship righted itself.

"I'm not sure we can fire many more blasts and have the ship hold together," Colwell said.

"I don't think we're going to have the option to. By my count, those are our last cannonballs," I said.

The shots struck the giant. Like before, the creature absorbed them, shook, and made its terrible wail. It seemed to slow it down some this time. Perhaps it had a finite amount of energy.

"We need to get right over the giant for Rhys to dump the rest of the contents of the anti-serum onto it. It's our last shot. We have to immobilize the creature," I said.

"That's going to be a lot harder than you make it sound," Ral said. "You're talking flying in low and hovering in place..."

"I believe in you," I said, looking him in the eye.

Ral nodded with determination. "Okay," he said, letting out a deep breath. "Let's do this."

I leaned over the funnel. "Someone make sure Rhys gets ready in the bottom aft compartment. I'm not sure he can hear me, even with the funnel," I said.

Our crew would handle the rest. They were reliable, and Lieutenant Ral was one of the best of them. His eyes were deadly serious as he set to the controls, lowering the nose of the *Liliana* into place. We drifted downward, closer to the giant as it moved. It had slowed from the hits, but it still posed a danger to our people. We couldn't let it keep going.

We were almost over the giant when it noticed us again. It darted to the side.

"Hang on," Ral said. He slammed on the controls.

The ship banked and rocked again, going nearly sideways, but Ral corrected with quick precision so we wouldn't tip all the way over. We were soon atop the giant. Ral maneuvered us slightly forward. Even though we were high enough off the ground not to be in danger, I never liked flying this low.

I gripped the handrail and looked through the telescope. The crew below would see when we were over the creature. All I could do was watch.

A blue substance poured out the back of the ship and, at first, it looked like it was going to miss the giant, but the creature ran right into it. It smoldered and smoked when it came into contact with the anti-serum. The liquid splashed on it, but then its skin absorbed it all into its body.

Instead of a screech, the giant roared in pain. The cry was so chilling I wished we didn't have to inflict it upon a creature. Nothing deserved that kind of torture.

The giant's face was like the ghost of a person, blank, except where its blue blood bubbled and pulsed. Perhaps once, the giant had full features, but whatever the Wyranth had done to it made it nothing but a monstrosity. I watched, holding my breath. Had our efforts with the anti-serum been fruitful?

The giant gave a start. It bent its knees and jumped, slamming the full force of its weight into the bottom of the *Liliana*. I couldn't believe it could jump that high, and gripped the handrail all the more tightly, pulling back from the telescope.

Our ship rocked. The rest of the windows of the bridge blew out, the glass shattering and flying everywhere. Wind flew through the cabin. My hair went wild and my knuckles turned white from my extreme grip on the rail.

The ship rattled again, and then jerked as the creature smashed another hole in it. Out on the deck, the crew screamed at each other as if there were anything we could do about the situation.

"Lieutenant Ral," I pleaded.

"I'm working on it. Your creature's stuck to our bottom, I think. Hold on. It's going to be a wild ride."

"All crew, brace for... unorthodox maneuvers," Colwell said into the communications funnel.

Several of the crew still on the deck scrambled for the mess to get inside.

I held on. Nothing could pry me from my handrail.

Ral pushed the controls all the way to the side. The ship wobbled from the strange weight below, and from the holes unbalancing the bottom of the ship. We began to spin, slowly at first, but then we gained speed like a top. With each rotation, we lifted further upward. I couldn't even look into the telescope to see if the maneuver worked. The rattling and the spinning made the world like a dizzying earthquake that never ended. It became impossible to see straight.

The creature released our hull, the weight differential causing one more shift to the piloting controls which sent us out of our spin with our nose pointing toward the ground. Gravity pulled us downward. Ral tried to steer us back level, but the controls didn't react fast enough. The bridge shot into the air. Even with the handrails, I could barely keep my footing.

"The damage is too severe and I pushed too hard. We're gonna crash!" Ral shouted.

No. This couldn't be happening. And there was little I could do but hang on for dear life. The nose kept falling toward the ground below, the ship wobbling into a spin. The propellers turned, but they couldn't get up to a speed high enough to keep us in the air.

The creature got to its feet in front of where we were headed.

Even if we survived the crash, the giant would still be out there, causing damage, rampaging through our people. It couldn't end like this. But what could I do?

"Can you direct the crash?" I shouted.

"I can try," Ral said, pushing on the controls.

"Drive us into the giant. We've slowed it down. Maybe the force of the ship can stop it."

"That's crazy." Ral shook his head and sucked in his breath. "But here we go." He jammed on the controls, turning the ship to the side.

My feet felt as if they were going to fly out from beneath me. My hands were sore from holding onto the rail so tightly. Commander Colwell held on just as tightly. His face turned a pale shade of white from the strain.

The *Liliana* veered to starboard, and soon the giant was in our sights. But our nose dove too quickly. We weren't going to be able to ram right into it.

The ground approached so rapidly, everything turned into a blur. The nose finally hit, mere feet from the giant. The momentum of the ship pushed the aft skyward, and we all lost our footing. I hung on.

The ship tipped forward, creaking and cracking from the strain. Several members of the crew cried out, both in fear and pain as not everyone had something firm to hold on to. I didn't want to look out onto the deck to see if my crew were going flying, but the weight turned my head for me, and I could see the deck falling toward the ground, shadows covering the earth. The giant turned, confused at what was going on.

Our turbines kept spinning, the propeller blades moving at rapid speed. Ral hadn't been able to turn them off in the middle of crashing. He had to brace for the impact as well, unable to free his hands to make any more maneuvers.

The ship tipped over, falling directly over the giant. It stood right under our forward turbine. The blades whirred and sliced into the giant as the full weight of the *Liliana* fell on it. Our blade cut the giant into shreds. Gelatinous blobs of shining blue goo shot everywhere. Pieces of the creature smacked into the bridge wall and onto the deck. It cried out in extreme agony, the loudest noise yet.

Soon enough, the sound came to a garbled stop. The weight of the *Liliana* crashed down, *booming* as the top of our ship collided with the ground. Dust shot in the air, covering everything. I lost my grip on the handle and fell to the roof of the bridge, which was now below my feet. Colwell and Ral dangled from the handrails at their stations above me.

The structure of the bridge wasn't enough to hold against the weight of the rest of the ship. The wooden columns cracked, and the ship crunched in on itself. I screamed.

The bridge collapsed entirely, wood splinters, debris, and dust flying everywhere. I fell to my knees and closed my eyes, wrapping my arms around my skull. Wooden debris dropped on me. It was heavy, hard. The weight forced me prone and into a knotted-up position where it hurt just to lay there. Colwell shouted something, but I couldn't understand it.

More weight fell atop me. I couldn't see anymore. My mind swam, whirling like the airship had been spinning moments prior. Darkness overcame me.

CHAPTER 28

It's been several minor skirmishes over the last few days. However, we received the worst news imaginable. King Malaky has been assassinated. How can this kingdom ever be the same?

An excerpt From Baron von Monocle's Log
Day 28 of the Month of the Fool
24th Year of King Malaky XV's Reign

"THERE SHE IS," a muffled male voice said.

Everything hurt so badly. My arms, my back, my legs. And I was in the most uncomfortable position possible. I wanted to retch from the pain. It smelled like dust and wood, and I found I couldn't move a muscle. The realization sent me into panic. What if I were paralyzed? My heart pounded. That only made matters worse, each heartbeat causing my head to throb as if it was a hammer driving me into the ground.

"She's under a lot of debris, everyone lift," another voice said. "On three. One, two..."

Men grunted, but the tremendous weight lifted. The pressure coming off me was freeing. I could breathe again. Though my body still hurt, and I still didn't want to move.

Whatever they had lifted crashed to the ground beside me, clanking against other wood. Someone touched me.

187

"She's breathing, but shallowly," this voice was feminine. Dr. du Clockhand?

"What do we do next, Doctor?" the male voice said, coming into focus. It sounded like Ethan.

The thought made me warm. It wasn't long ago I had feared never seeing him again. Now, if only I could muster the strength to open my eyes. I tried, and the world I saw was terribly out of focus. It was dimly lit, but everything was a blur.

"Zaira?" Dr. du Clockhand asked with a gentle touch to my back. "Don't move too quickly. You've been gravely injured and you need to take it slow."

Gravely injured? What happened?

I recalled the crash. The memory came flooding back to me. The second time I'd crashed the *Liliana*. This time, at least, was a part of the battle. But what happened? Was that the end of the creature? I'd witnessed it torn to pieces by our turbines, but I needed to know what happened afterward.

Despite all the pain in me, I tried to sit up. Without the big weight on me, it proved a little bit easier, though my back was so sore, bruised all over. I clenched my teeth to fight the pain.

Dr. du Clockhand assisted me to a seated position. "You're so stubborn," she said. "Please, don't rush yourself. I told you already to take it slow."

I still couldn't see clearly. I took a couple of deep breaths, slow ones, trying to center myself. My eyes finally came into focus. We were in the dark, the broken ship all around us. A couple of soldiers carried handheld gas lamps. Dr. du Clockhand knelt next to me, hands folded in her lap. Several men stood around us with swords and pistols at their hips—knights. I recognized Cid, and then I spotted Ethan.

His face was tight, full of concern. He relaxed somewhat when our eyes connected.

How I'd missed seeing his beautiful face. I never wanted to be apart from it again. It stilled my breath, which made the pain in my ribs flare. I winced. "Okay," I said weakly, "can someone tell me what happened?" I stifled a breath. "Is Toby okay? My ferret."

Dr. du Clockhand lightly touched my shoulder. "Your ferret made it. He's with Rhys, who returned to Cliffside Castle to get rest and recover in a more suitable environment. As far as what happened..."

Ethan stepped forward. "I can only tell you my account of what happened from below. I'm sure you know what happened on the airship as well as anyone else," he said.

"Yeah," I said, unable to nod.

"You saw the giant blob creature," Ethan said. "It came out of the forest. Some of the army scouts found its location. We captured some of the Wyranth stationed there after they brought it to our attention.

I rubbed my shoulder. It had a sore spot that was tight and I couldn't quite get to relax.

Ethan continued, "Part of the reason for their pushing so deep into Rislandia was to try to secure the remaining giant locations. Their spies had been aware of our earthquakes and tracked the epicenters to determine the locations of the two we found in our country. The soldiers were willing to fight hard to get access to the serum again. They secured the first outside of Plainsroad Village, as you already know." He nodded toward me.

"Yeah," I said, trying to stretch my back.

"The Iron Emperor insisted on ensuring they had a second means of production, as a backup in case we managed to take out the first. He's really good at long-term planning. They found that in the forest. Simultaneously, Wyranth scientists were working on ways to do more with the serum to help turn the Wyranth into a super army. They inadvertently discovered ways to morph the giant back into something closer to its prior form. It wasn't intentional. Once informed of it, however, the Iron Emperor wanted them to proceed with the experiment, in hopes that these giants might be the key to tilting the scales of the war once and for all."

The talk of the Iron Emperor made me cringe. He was probably out there, waltzing around Rislandia trying to bend our people to his whims.

"I was on the battlefield when the *Liliana* arrived," Ethan said but crouched in front of me. "I was happy to see you since the fight wasn't going well. The Wyranth had both numbers and superior power. If the battle was going to be attrition, we were going to lose. But you sprayed the chemical across their ranks. It did a lot of good. A large number of the Wyranth lost their fighting spirit and fled, just like we planned. The whole thing turned into chaos with Wyranth running left and right, and even though they were in trouble, it looked for a moment like we were going to be overrun by their remaining forces.

He took a deep breath. "And then that thing came out of the forest. I know we saw one of them in the mine, but with it moving around, its arms waving and legs stomping..." Ethan shook his head. "It's frightening. I was nearly trampled by it, but Cid pulled me out of the way."

Cid inclined his head but didn't seem smug over the praise.

Ethan acknowledged him with a small, thankful smile. "But the airship... how did you make it crash right into the creature like that? You ripped it!"

I moistened my lips, my mouth so dry I could hardly part them. How long had I been out? I had so many questions. "Luck," I managed to say.

"Von Monocle luck," Dr. du Clockhand said, as if it were a fact of life.

Ethan looked at me curiously. "Maybe it's true."

"I don't know," I said. "I just want to be out of here. What's happening now?"

Cid cleared his throat. "We are pressing the attack forward now that we have the momentum. The Wyranth are in disarray and our main force is heading toward Rislandia City."

"I want to go," I said, sitting up a little straighter. The movement made my skull throb. I brought my hand to my forehead.

"Zaira, don't move so much. There's no way you can go back into a fight after that crash. It's amazing you're alive at all."

My eyes widened. "What about the crew?"

Ethan and Cid looked at each other, quiet for a moment. Their somber faces were telling. "Well," Ethan said.

"You sustained several casualties," Cid said. "Less than one would have anticipated from a crash, but I'm sorry, Baron von Monocle. At least fifteen of your crew are dead or unaccounted for."

The news stung. So many friends and colleagues lost. I wanted to cry, but my tear ducts were too dry. The thought of loss reminded me of the journal we'd been carrying. Those contained plans. I tensed. We had to find that journal. It would be so important, but my mouth was so dry I could hardly speak. I needed a drink. "Water," I said.

Dr. du Clockhand scuffled through her bag and pushed a canteen to my lips. The water hit them and gave me instant relief. I sipped it slowly at first, but then chugged, taking the canteen into my own hands. I nearly drained half of it before setting down, stopping to catch breath. "I was so thirsty," I said.

"Understandable. You've been stuck here for several hours without water," Dr. du Clockhand said.

"There's a journal here, somewhere in the ship. It contains schematics and designs for different aerial vessels," I said, glancing around. "We need to recover it."

"I'll get a team on it," Cid said. He nodded to one of his knights, who departed in haste. Hopefully they would be able to find it.

I couldn't worry anymore about the journal for now. There was still so much to do. I pushed myself to my feet. If my ship were down for the count, and several of my crew were dead, the last thing I was going to do was sit around and think about it. Getting depressed did no one any good.

Ethan jutted up from his crouch, and so did Dr. du Clockhand. They each gripped one of my arms as if I were liable to fall and shatter. I shook them off. "I can stand. I'm fine."

As I said the words, pain shot up my leg and through my lower back. I couldn't help but wince.

"You're not fine," Dr. du Clockhand insisted.

"I'm well enough that I can march," I said, narrowing my eyes.

Ethan stepped back. "I know when she's like this, and I'm not going to argue with her."

Cid narrowed his eyes in contemplation for a long moment but finally grunted an agreement. "It would make for a good symbolic moment for a von Monocle to lead the charge into Rislandia City."

"It would," I said. Cid had just validated what I wanted to do. Before I could embrace the full feeling of triumph, however, it made me worry about other things. "My father, is he...?"

I let the words linger. The knights looked between each other. "He is with the general army, but I haven't heard any word that he's been injured or missing. No doubt he will be charging along with the forces," Cid said.

"Which means we don't need Zaira for the symbol," Ethan said. He sounded so defensive.

It made my blood boil, but I took a slow breath to calm myself. The only reason he said that was to protect me. Should I chastise him or be grateful he cared so much about me? I didn't need to be babied.

"I've already made the decision. I'm going," I said. "We have to take the city back. If we don't, there's no Rislandia and no point in having worked this hard or sacrificed this much. It sounds like we need to leave soon to catch up with the army. Let's get out of here and see if any of the rest of the crew want to join us."

"I don't give you a clean bill of health," Dr. du Clockhand said, "but your mental faculty is certainly still here, and given the circumstances, I have to say you're right."

Instead of saying more, I motioned Cid to lead the way.

The knight moved, making his way through the back wall of the bridge where someone had cut a hole big enough for a person to slip through to the outside.

I was surprised to find it was light out when I exited the death trap that was formerly my airship. I must have been buried under enough debris that no light filtered in from the outside. I squinted to allow my eyes to adjust. The *Liliana* blocked most of the view to the east, but to the west I could see the thick trees of the Old Forest, with the red sun setting over the horizon. The plains to the south were burnt, most of the fires from the battle out by now, but some smoke still rose from the plains. Bodies littered the field. Several members of the army lifted their fallen compatriots into carts. The sight made me choke.

Gasping made matters worse. The air wasn't fresh at all, but had a foul, rotten smell from all the death and burning. The Wyranth had done far too much harm, but we finally had a chance to reverse the course of the war.

A good portion of their soldiers would be on the run. They would have those intense feelings from the anti-serum for a few more days at the best, but it would also have cured them completely of their driving rage from the monster's blood they'd been ingesting. If everything had gone according to plan. All we had was Rhys's theory to go upon, and so little had worked out in our favor as of late.

I walked southward. My head felt like it was about to fall off, and my stomach churned from the pain. The lack of rest was catching up to me, but I had to march.

Several of the remaining crew saw me. Even covered in dirt, with my cape ripped from the impact of all the debris, I stood out on the battlefield like a sore thumb. The red drew eyes like a magnet, though my blouse was dirtied enough it would unlikely be the bright white it used to be. Everyone else wore the same uniform. I was a beacon in the sea of gray.

One by one, several soldiers stood from where they were sitting, whether it be at medical tents or with others. They followed me. I kept charging forward, and before long, there were more than a hundred soldiers and knights at my back. I stopped to turn. Some of them were my crew, some of them I didn't recognize, but they all looked to me to lead them and give them inspiration.

I'd done this before with my own crew. I could do it again. My hand tightened into a ball, clutching onto my cape. For the first time, I held the bottom of the cape toward the soldiers. "I know we're all tired and hungry. We miss our families. We've had so much loss these last few weeks. But do you see this cape? When I first saw it, I thought it looked stupid, foolish. Who would put a big red target on their back in the middle of a battle?"

Several people chuckled.

I paced in front of them. "My father did. And he did so despite it marking him. Because it told the enemy, 'I'm not afraid of you.' We've been running in fear of the Wyranth for too long, falling back while they destroy everything we held dear. But with our source of power..." I paused to point to the airship, "...we took down *their* source of power. This marks a new moment for us as a people. We can overcome anything."

A few soldiers began to clap, and then all of them erupted into a cheer. I couldn't help but smile, even though the tightening of my cheek muscles made my head hurt worse.

I released my cape and held my fist in the air. "It's time to fight for Rislandia!"

Another roar of a cheer erupted, and the men moved forward. They weren't marching slowly behind me anymore, but they took off like a stampeding herd. I turned, and though my legs were fine, I wasn't sure if I could maintain that speed. I did the best I could anyway, trudging forward. My body ached too much to run. Despite the rousing speech, I wasn't going to be able to keep up with the soldiers.

The army continued on ahead of me. They had a cause. I was expected to be toward the back anyway. If I were honest with myself, my presence at the head of the battle proper wouldn't be all that important. I'd probably just get in the way.

Resigned to lagging behind, I dropped my pace to a slow walk. The scorched plains beneath me made for a depressing sight, even still. All the energy I'd gained from my speech evaporated.

But then something let out a loud *honk* behind me. I turned to see a horseless carriage, a four-seater with a steam stack protruding from the middle, wheels with white painted spokes, and Ethan von Lantern sitting in the driver's seat. Behind him sat Cid, and another knight occupied the second back seat. The front was open.

"Hop in," Ethan said.

"Where did you find this?" I asked.

"The knights have our ways," Ethan said, grinning. "You've given us enough rides on your airship, now you can ride in our style."

I opened the side door and slipped into the leather seat. It felt good to sit down. I shut the door behind me. "The small blessings," I said to myself.

"Hmm?" Ethan asked, cocking his head to hear me over the whir of the engine.

He didn't need to know it was hard for me to walk. I pointed forward instead. "I said, let's go retake Rislandia City!"

CHAPTER 29

The crew's resolve is stronger than ever. We will finish off the Wyranth for the sake of our fallen king. The Wyranth will not triumph.

An excerpt From Baron von Monocle's Log
Day 30 of the Month of the Fool
24th Year of King Malaky XV's Reign

WE CAUGHT UP to the marching troops in no time at all. Ethan slowed the horseless carriage to putter alongside those walking. After about an hour of riding, the Crystal Spire appeared in the distance, followed by the city walls. Smoke rose from the city proper. Though there was bound to be damage from the way the Wyranth ransacked prior cities, seeing that they hadn't toppled the spire brought me hope. The symbol of our existence still stood. If the palace survived, we would have the basics we needed to reestablish ourselves in our city.

Gunfire interrupted our parade. The soldiers fanned out, taking positions while we lingered behind in the horseless carriage. Up ahead, several Wyranth soldiers were down in bunkers, firing at us. They didn't have any artillery backup, thankfully, and we vastly outnumbered them.

Still, it didn't prevent casualties on our side. Two soldiers went down when our group stormed the bunker, but we managed to overtake it and take down the Wyranth soldiers.

They didn't go down without a vicious fight. These Wyranth hadn't received the anti-serum, and they were as ferocious as any I'd ever come across. I felt guilty watching from the carriage, but I needed to reserve what little energy I had for when we entered the city.

The enemy's presence was a reminder that there was going to be a lot more to this fight than these few battles, even if these were ones we had to win for our survival. Our soldiers managed to capture one of the Wyranth alive, who struggled even as he was brought to the back.

I stepped out of the carriage. I wanted to see the enemy face to face and find out if there was any information I could get about the city. Cid followed but told Ethan to stay in the driver's seat so we could move quickly when the time came. I walked to the prisoner, who was being held by two burly Rislandian men, and circled by a dozen more. The Wyranth squirmed and tried to bite at his captors.

Marina was close by, blending into the crowd in her uniform. She stepped forward when she saw me. "He won't be any use in interrogation. The serum makes some of us go a bit crazy in the head," she said. "It depends on a person's fortitude."

"We have to try," I said.

"And then what do we do with him?" one of the soldiers asked.

I didn't have a good answer to his question. I didn't want to hurt an innocent prisoner, but we couldn't take him with us. I looked to Cid for guidance.

The older knight narrowed his eyes. "We knock him out and make sure there's no weapons left around him. There's little harm he can do on his own for now," he said.

Satisfied, I stepped forward.

The Wyranth had dark hair and bloodshot eyes. He'd been battling hard for too long, just like the rest of us. He hadn't shaved in several days, his face a mess of longer hair, smattered with dirt. He had a bruise under his left eye from the fisticuffs with our soldiers.

"Hello," I said.

"You're not going to win. Turn yourself into the Iron Emperor and beg for his mercy!" the Wyranth spat.

"Things have changed now," I said. "There's no more serum."

The Wyranth twitched and turned his head to the side.

"Tell us about Rislandia City. Are there many forces still there?" I asked. "You heard my people. We're going to be merciful to you."

"It doesn't matter," the Wyranth said.

"Why?"

"You don't know what the Iron Emperor has planned. He still has his scientists. He still has our superior people. You won't be able to stop us." The Wyranth broke into a chilling laugh. He glanced at all of us as if *we* were the prisoners and he was the ones interrogating us. "Nothing you do matters."

"Shut him up," Marina said, fire in her eyes. She stepped ahead of me, and I let her through. Interrogating prisoners was not my expertise. I never wanted it to be something I'd get good at. She had... fewer scruples than I did.

Marina backhanded the Wyranth soldier across his face. "You're lucky the baronette is in charge here, or you'd be shaking in your boots, even with the serum coursing through your blood. Now answer the woman."

The Wyranth solder kept laughing. Marina struck him again, harder this time.

His head jolted from the blow, and when he righted himself, blood trickled from his lip, mixing with spittle, forming a long bead of bloody drool that hung past his chin. He spat it to the ground. "It doesn't matter. We sacked your city and moved on. You'll not find many of us there, but you have no idea what's coming. No idea!"

Marina lifted her hand to strike him a third time.

All of these Wyranth soldiers seemed to say the same thing. But did this one know we already destroyed the giant creature? There'd be no way to find out quickly. He'd inadvertently given us some good information—the city wouldn't be heavily defended. "That's enough," I said.

Marina turned to look at me. All of the soldiers had their eyes on me, expectant.

"We don't need to torture our prisoners. We aren't them. He's told us what we needed to know. Let's follow Cid's plan." I spun on my feet, letting my red cape flow behind me. "Knock him out and let's get moving. We can't waste time. Every moment could mean Rislandian lives."

Cid turned and followed after me, his long strides catching up with me quickly. I heard the *crack* of a rifle butt against skull from behind me, something I was grateful not to have to watch. The soldiers would follow my lead. It energized me to know that. All the pain I'd endured, it escaped me.

"You did well," Cid said. "I rarely see leadership capabilities so strong."

His words of praise made me crack a small smile. "Thank you," I said.

We returned to the carriage and pressed forward with our band of soldiers. When we approached the gate, the sun was setting. Cid spotted a large force of people coming from the forest. He produced a spyglass and looked intently, seeming worried. If it were the Wyranth, it would all be over. This would be for naught, as we couldn't manage to fight a large force.

More and more soldiers poured from the forest, such a large mass I'd rarely seen outside of parades or from the air when I looked down upon a battle. They loomed and moved closer to us.

"They don't have the Wyranth helms. It's our people!" Cid said. He set the spyglass down and leaned back into his chair. "By Malaky, that gave me a worry."

"At least we could have tried to flee in the carriage if it had been the Wyranth," Ethan said.

"Everyone halt!" I shouted to the soldiers up front. The men followed my orders, and a small ambassadorial group holding a flag with the crest of King Malaky came forward from the group in the forest.

I left the carriage again. The contingent would want to meet with me, as I'd become the leader of this group. Cid should have been directing them, but he deferred to me. It was probably more for the symbol of it as Cid would help most with the correct fighting tactics but, regardless, I needed to do my duty.

Three soldiers peeled away from my group to give me an adequate honor guard, and we paced toward the flag bearer, meeting them in the tall grasses off of the road. It was dark by the time we arrived, and I couldn't make out any faces.

"Ho there!" One of them called. "Name and rank?"

I recognized the voice immediately. My father. "Father?" I asked.

"Zaira?" His voice changed from deep to a high-pitched question. Love and compassion replaced formality. He ran forward and wrapped me in an embrace.

My ribs hurt from the contact, and it made me wince. "I'm a little tender," I told him.

My father stepped back to give me space. "The airship crash," he said. "I saw it from a distance. I wanted to look in on you, but I had to get our forces organized for an assault on the city. The Wyranth scattered just like we planned. Well done, Zaira! Unfortunately, so did our army. I gathered who I could find with the help of some others, and we retreated into the forest to regroup. We took the route through the forest so any eagle-eyed Wyranth wouldn't spot us. You must have taken a more direct route to catch up?"

I nodded. "There aren't many of us. So, the Wyranth can't be prepared for a large attack if they spotted us."

"Good. They always underestimate us. That is their weakness. Oh, it gives me so much relief to know you survived the crash." He placed his hand on his chest. "At my age, such stress can be bad for my health. At least, that's what Talyen tells me."

I laughed. He always kept such a light-hearted spirit. It was inspiring. "Well, it's nightfall. It would be a good time to launch a surprise attack."

"That it would," my father said. He turned toward the city walls. "My men are ready. Yours should integrate with ours and fall back into their units."

"Sounds good," I said. I felt better not having this major battle rest on my shoulders. We had the full strength of the army with my father in charge. Finally, things were going right. Here I'd thought my von Monocle luck had run dry.

"Grab your men, tell them to slip into the forest and—"

Before he could utter another word, cannon fire launched into my soldiers on the road. I turned to see the blasts. They came from the walls of the city itself. The Wyranth had the city defended after all. The skies sparked as more cannons fired their payloads in our direction. Soldiers cried out as the blasts struck. One direct hit after another. My people scattered and screamed.

I turned, grateful it was dark and that I couldn't see the damage done. "Run for the forest! Take cover!" I shouted to my people.

They didn't need to be told a second time. More cannon blasts exploded in our direction. Those who survived ran for their lives.

CHAPTER 30

We won the battle, but there is still much fighting to do. My dear friend will soon ascend as King Malaky XVI, but he does not wish to do so until the new year, and until the Wyranth are completely driven from our land.

An excerpt From Baron von Monocle's Log
Day 38 of the Month of the Fool
24th Year of King Malaky XV's Reign

ALL OF US ran into the cover of the trees. It didn't stop the cannonballs from coming, but they couldn't target us as easily. A large oak cracked as a cannonball rammed into its trunk, collapsing to the forest floor. I was out of breath from moving so quickly and placed my hands on my hips. We couldn't linger for long. "What do we do now?" I asked my father.

"Same thing we were going to do before. We can't let a few cannons stop us," my father said.

"Tell the cannons that," I said.

My father turned, peering toward the city. There wasn't much of a view to be had through the thick trees. "We split our forces between the north and west entrances to the city," my father said, now speaking loud enough as if shouting commands to his soldiers.

The soldiers formed up around us as another volley of cannonballs flew into the forest. Those shots landed at least thirty feet away. It meant the Wyranth didn't have a good look at us. They were guessing with their fire.

"The gates will be open," my father said. "They've been made stationary since the invention of the horseless carriage to allow traffic to flow. We can rush in through both of those and, hopefully, catch the cannoneers on the top walls off guard. Has anyone been stationed on city guard duty here?"

A number of the soldiers raised their hands.

"I want you to head in through the north so you can make your way into the walls and take the cannons. Colonel Rennie will lead that contingent through," my father said. "Everyone else, let's head through the western gate. I doubt they'll be manning cannons there, as they've taken most of the cities to the west. We'll form a pincer attack and converge on King Malaky's palace."

Mutters of agreement came from all around me.

My father clapped his hands together. "Let's go!"

Soldiers took off running toward both gates, hustling through the forest. I moved carefully alongside my father so as not to inadvertently run into someone.

Ethan soon came to my side and linked his arm with mine. "I'm coming with you," he said.

My father turned around and saw the two of us touching. "What..." He shook his head, looking more flustered than I'd ever seen him. "Let's go," he said, more gruffly than usual.

I turned bright red. Ethan taking my arm had felt so natural I didn't even think to question the implications or people seeing it. By Malaky, we'd been together so often on the airship I'd forgotten there was any propriety left to uphold. And the way my father looked at me with such judgment... He had no right to even think that way, with the way he and Talyen acted aboard the *Liliana* for so long. Oh, it drove me mad.

Ethan must have sensed how flustered I was. He pulled his arm softly away from me. "Sorry," he said in a near whisper.

I didn't acknowledge him but, instead, ran after my father. There were more important things than our budding relationship. This was just another complication I didn't need to distract me.

We reached the edge of the forest, circling around the river until we came to one of the stone walking bridges built more than a hundred years ago. It only allowed a few of us across at a time, but we lined up and crossed. My father had been right, the Wyranth didn't guard the western entrance, figuring it would be safe from any advance.

Our soldiers had their guns at the ready as they charged. I produced my pistol from its holster and followed. Everyone was quiet, boots pattering across the cobblestone road when we reached the main gate. We rushed into the city, into the industrial district, where the machines had all stopped. Production was dead. Several of the buildings were burned down and many of the gas lamps were out. It was dark and quiet, though gunfire echoed from the northern part of the city.

My father waved his arm like a windmill to tell the soldiers to keep advancing. We pushed through the industrial district until we came across a Wyranth patrol. We outnumbered them ten to one, but the Wyranth had grenades.

Two of the Wyranth soldiers chucked their grenades in our direction. They rolled to the front line of our soldiers and exploded, taking out five of our men. Our soldiers immediately opened fire, gunning down the Wyranth in the streets. I couldn't help but wince at all the violence.

There was something different about aerial combat, firing into faceless masses so distant. It wasn't quite as disturbing as being up close to bloodshed. It froze me. In the course of the battle, I hadn't fired a single bullet.

"I don't know what's going on with you," Ethan said in a low voice, the barrel of his gun still smoking as he lowered it to his side, "but we're going to need your help, Zaira."

I didn't know what was wrong with me, either. I'd been in combat situations before, but I'd seen too much death in the last several days. How did the others not feel the same way? I didn't say anything because I didn't want to cause any trouble or influence the battle negatively. But there could be hundreds or more Wyranth between us and King Malaky's palace. I tried to keep my eyes forward so I wouldn't see the extent of the wounds just inflicted. I couldn't think about it or it would make things worse. We had an objective to accomplish, and Ethan was right, I had to do my part.

The soldiers moved forward, faster than before. They could taste the victory. It was so close, and we needed it so badly. Even if we'd lost so much, having the city back would mean more to Rislandians than anything else we could accomplish.

We rounded a street corner, passing some shops with broken windows. The Wyranth had ransacked all the supplies from several stores around us. Glass littered the ground. It was terrible to see the city in disrepair, but I looked to the sky. The spire still watched over us, unharmed, a constant reminder of who we were. Light emanated from the top of it, shining a soft illumination over the city, which would have been completely covered in the darkness of night otherwise.

The palace came into view. We were almost there.

Bullets flew from the darkness of the streets ahead.

Four of our soldiers spun and fell as gunshots rang out. I pointed my gun around, but I couldn't see where the Wyranth had fired from. Gunshot sounds echoed through the near empty streets, adding to the confusion.

Ethan flung himself onto me, pushing me to the side of the street and in through one of the broken shop windows. "You're too much of a target with that cape of yours," he said. "Stay hidden."

The room looked like an old inn's common room, with several tables, a wooden bar, and modern brass appliances. Ethan flipped one of the tables on its side. "Duck behind this," he said.

Even as the shots kept firing outside, I fretted about my father, who was still exposed to the Wyranth in the streets. I tried my best to find him through the inn's broken windows. Out of the corner of my eye, I caught a glimpse of my father moving toward the palace. He had several commandos around him still, but he was in danger.

"I see one of the Wyranth," Ethan said. "I'm going to sneak up on him." He crouched and made his way through the room and out another broken window, leaving me alone.

I stayed behind the table for a while, despite hearing cries of pain and more gunshots. The last few minutes were such a whirl. Ethan had told me to fight, and then he told me to hide. Which did he want? And did it even matter? I had to take control of my own destiny.

But it was so strange being here without my crew. I felt naked without them. The army was fighting with me, but they weren't *my* people. I was more alone in this battle than I'd been in some time.

No. This was wrong. I shouldn't be the one hiding and working myself into a scared frenzy. I gripped my pistol more tightly and peeked over the top of the table. Most of the army had gone ahead. I saw no sign of Ethan or my father.

A few figures ran toward the palace. Their metal helmets shined in the light cast down from the street lamps and the Crystal Spire. Wyranth.

This was my chance. If I could move quickly, I would be able to stop the Wyranth from coming up behind the Rislandians. We wouldn't get anywhere if we were ambushed.

I moved with slow steps toward the window. In the shadows, no one could see me, or my bright red cape for that matter. I held my pistol out, extending my arms so I could get a good view and hold it steady. There were three enemies. The middle one stood perfectly in my sights.

I pulled the trigger.

The gunshot blasted—a clean hit into the Wyranth's back. He fell to the ground, but the other two Wyranth turned. They saw where the shot had come from and fired in my direction. I ducked below the window opening, narrowly avoiding the shots from their rifles. I could hear their boots stomping toward me. Two on one wasn't good odds, even with my cover. I needed to take one of them down if I had any possibility of surviving.

In a quick movement, I lifted my gun and looked out through the opening. I didn't have time to take aim with the soldiers already having their guns trained in my direction. I fired another shot and ducked, not looking to see if I hit.

One of the Wyranth moaned in pain. I must have struck true. More confident, I tried to fire again.

Only one was standing now, as both were wounded, but he fired as soon as I popped up. His shot blasted right into my gun, propelling it out of my hands. My hands felt like they were burning up, and I shook them, but ducked immediately. Now I had no weapon. What could I do?

The Wyranth edged closer, his footsteps pattering on the cobblestone outside. "You killed my comrades, and you're going to suffer," the man said, his voice deep and gritty. He cocked his rifle. The sound was so close he must have made his way over, but I couldn't risk moving from my cover.

The barrel of a rifle appeared right in front of my face. I dove to the side, rolling. The rifle blasted, smashing the tiles of the floor where I had been a moment prior.

I screamed, scrambling to my feet. The Wyranth cocked his gun again.

I zigzagged back and forth to try to make it difficult to aim. What could I do? I couldn't overpower a muscular male soldier, and there was nowhere for me to run.

"Stay still, girl. You've been too much trouble already," the Wyranth said.

A shot fired, and in the same instant, I closed my eyes. I was done for but, oddly, I didn't feel any pain.

When I opened my eyes again, I saw the Wyranth soldier falling face forward to the floor. My heart raced so fast it seemed like it would explode. I tried to take deep breaths to calm myself.

Standing behind where the Wyranth had been was Ethan, a smoking pistol in his hand. He'd shot the Wyranth at point blank range. "Are you okay?" he asked, eyes shining.

"Yeah," I said, nearly breathless. He'd just saved my life. I would have been helpless if it wasn't for him. I sucked in my bottom lip to moisten it. My lips were so dry. "We should head to the palace now."

Ethan nodded. "I think it's clear back here. Good thing we were here or our people might have been sniped from behind."

"Good thing," I agreed, though I felt it was more a good thing he was here for me. True, I'd just taken down two of the other Wyranth, but it felt insignificant compared to my having been moments from death.

Ethan offered his hand, helping me step through the window opening and back onto the cobblestone street. Several shots fired in the distance, along with something that sounded like an explosion. We had to trust the rest of the army were doing their jobs.

When I was through, he released me and bent down by one of the Wyranth I had shot. He picked up one of their rifles. Then, he tossed his pistol to me. "Probably better for you to have the lighter weapon. Just don't lose it. Okay?"

I caught the pistol. Ethan was so observant to note I didn't have a pistol in my hand. Those little observations and quick-wittedness differentiated a knight from other soldiers. One day, when we were out of this, I hoped we'd have a lot of good little observations together. For now, we had more work to do.

We paced toward the palace, and then broke into a jog. The rest of our group would be ahead of us. The palace doors were open. Bodies littered the hallway into the main chambers where I'd met my father and King Malaky so many times. Several of the wall tapestries were ruined, vases cracked and destroyed. So much beauty tarnished because the Wyranth couldn't leave our poor kingdom alone.

I carefully stepped over one of our own soldiers, who had fallen, frowning at the sight. I heard voices speaking ahead of us. "I think they're in the war room," I whispered.

Ethan kept by my side as we progressed further into the palace into the big room with open double doors. Inside stood several of our soldiers, weapons pointed at Wyranth, who in turn had their weapons pointed back at them. A stalemate, about equal numbers.

"General Swift," my father said, apparently recognizing the man standing in front of him. "You have an untenable situation here. You've fought quite a war, I have to hand it to you, but it's time to lay down your arms and surrender."

"Never," the Wyranth general said. He wore the same uniform as his colleagues, but no helmet with their epic points atop them. His uniform was adorned with many colorful ribbons. He had a gaunt face with a goatee.

"More Rislandians!" one of the other Wyranth soldiers shouted. All of the Wyranth guns turned toward us.

The movement spooked one of the Rislandians, who opened fire. He shot the gun right out of General Swift's hand.

The Wyranth fired back. Soon bullets flew everywhere. Ethan tackled me to force me to the ground. We had desks and tables between us and the Wyranth soldiers, as well as the larger table that had the tactical map of the Areth continent. Several of our soldiers went down. So did some of the Wyranth.

I could make out the legs of some of the Wyranth soldiers and took initiative, firing Ethan's pistol. My shot connected, sending the Wyranth stumbling and limping. Our soldiers finished him off.

I scrambled away from Ethan as we kept our guns firing like the furnace of a steam engine to keep pressure on the Wyranth. Remembering how our tactics worked in the giant's cavern in the mine outside Plainsroad Village, I crawled around to flank the remaining Wyranth.

In the confusion, I didn't see another of the Wyranth sneaking around to do the same against us. I found myself face to face with General Swift himself. My eyes went wide. He moved with incredible speed, wrapping his arm around my stomach and pulling me close to him before I could react. He was a lot bigger than me, and even though I struggled as best I could, there was little I could do against his prowess.

Swift stood, forcing me along with him. "Everyone, cease fire!" he shouted.

His arm clenched around my stomach, barely allowing me enough room to breathe. When he pulled me closer, I nearly choked. In his other arm, he produced a knife and held it to my neck. "General von Monocle, I have your daughter. If you want her to live, you will let us go."

My father narrowed his eyes at the enemy general, but he held his arm out, his palm open. He wanted the others to stop. Even though he kept the most stoic of faces, I could see the worry in his eyes. They nearly twitched with anticipation. "Don't bring a girl into this," my father said.

"She is a combatant like anyone else here," Swift said, nearly spitting his words.

The knife grazed my skin, I couldn't help but wince.

My reaction made the Rislandians in the room squirm. They trained their weapons on Swift.

"If I die, so does she," Swift said.

My father wouldn't risk me, despite the fact that he should have just had the other men shoot the Wyranth general. What did I matter in the scheme of saving Rislandia? I wished I'd been stronger, able to resist the man holding me, but strength wasn't my gift.

My stubbornness and fighting spirit, however, were. This Wyranth needed me alive or he'd never make it out of the palace. It meant he couldn't do real harm to me. While others in the room might not risk a shot, I could act.

I picked up my foot and slammed it down hard on General Swift's toes.

Even though he wore heavy boots like most military officers, my movement was enough to inflict pain. He cried out and stumbled back. His blade grazed my neck, but it didn't cut deep as it fell. "You... you..."

His movement loosened his arm from my neck, and I was able to duck out of his grip, dropping to the floor. "Fire!" I screamed, hoping the Rislandians would react quickly.

Several gunshots rang out at once. At this close range and indoors, the sound was loud enough to make my ears ring. The smell of gunpowder filled the room.

The Wyranth fell atop me, the full weight of the larger man pressing down on my back. Memories of the airship crash filled me. It felt as if a great weight were descending upon me, constricting my neck and preventing me from breathing, as if the entire bridge had collapsed again, leaving me buried under the rubble. I screamed. My already sore body ached from the extra abuse. I became dizzy, my vision fogging in front of me. I wanted to scream, but I couldn't.

Several boots came into my view. "Get the scum off her," Ethan said. He bent down with two other soldiers and rolled my former captor's body aside.

Freed from the weight, I pushed myself to my knees.

Ethan brought me into a tight embrace. "Zaira! I thought you were done for. By Malaky..." he trailed off. Tears were in his eyes. He pulled my face to his chest.

Being next to him felt like curling up next to the stove back home in Plainsroad Village. I shivered despite the comfort of his warmth. I could hear his heart beating in his chest, pounding just like mine. I couldn't process what had just happened. There had been too much death, too many instances where I'd almost died. One of these times, my luck was going to run out in earnest and it would be the end of me.

"The palace is clear," one of the soldiers announced.

"Victory!" my father shouted. "Rislandia City is ours!"

211

All of the soldiers cheered, but I stayed on the floor of the war room for a long time, allowing Ethan to hold me.

EPILOGUE

DOCTORS ORDERED ME out of the action for the next several days, giving me an alchemic brew of painkillers to ease me into rest. I was still tender and bruised from all of the beating I'd taken from the airship collapsing on me.

I had been running on pure adrenaline during the Second Battle of Rislandia City, as people were now calling it. Though there was so much more to do, I was too weary to protest the doctors' orders. I fell asleep in one of the palace's guest rooms, just as I had in my visit after first encountering the Wyranth.

I drifted in and out of sleep for days. Ethan came to visit several times. Once, when I was still asleep, he woke me with a kiss to my forehead. "I'm sorry, Zaira. I have to return to my duties with the knights, and I can't stay with you any longer, but you'll be fine. I'll see you when you're well."

I was too tired to do anything but smile, and I fell right back asleep. This time, I dreamed of being in King Malaky's court, wearing the ugly hunter green ball of poofs and ruffles that most of the nobility wore in his presence. James and Ethan were there, and we had a banquet together. It was nice. Pleasant. Warm.

When I woke from the dream, my energy had returned. I wanted nothing more than to get up and find out exactly what I'd missed while being bedridden. Was the city being rebuilt? Was our army pressing farther south? What was to become of the crashed airship? I had so many questions and hollered for the nurses to fetch me clothes so I could get out of bed.

Dr. du Clockhand came to my room. She hadn't been among the doctors who first saw to me, as she had to attend to the wounded back on the battlefield between Cliffside Castle and the city. But she was here now, smiling. "You overexerted yourself, Baronette."

I shrugged. The motion still made my shoulders sore, but it wasn't nearly as bad as it had been the first days after the battle. "I did what needed to be done," I said.

"We all did," Dr. du Clockhand said, moving to my side. She brought out a stethoscope, placing two ends in the ears and the metal end under my gown, pressing to my back. It was cold and made me jolt at first. "You're breathing okay," she observed.

"I would hope so," I said, taking in a few deeper breaths after she brought it to my attention.

She removed the stethoscope and stepped back from my bed. "You still should take it easy for a few more days. No rushing into action," she said.

"I don't have an airship to rush to," I said with a wry smile.

"That didn't stop you last time, did it?"

She had me there. I didn't say anything for a long moment. Both of us broke into laughter.

"I'm glad you're okay," Dr. du Clockhand said.

Someone knocked on the door, and then Harkerpal peeked his head into the room. "Are visitors allowed?"

"Of course," Dr. du Clockhand said, motioning him inside.

Harkerpal stepped in, revealing a big bouquet of elegant red flowers in a glass vase. "There's so few places in our poor country that aren't war torn, these were difficult to find," Harkerpal said. "Have I told you about the time where your father set out to find the rarest flower in the world and bring it to your dear mother for their anniversary? We sailed all the way to the Dragonmist Isles. Those islands didn't get their name for nothing!" He bobbed his head several times as he spoke, moving to set down the vase on the nightstand. "We found several large bone structures on the beaches there. We know giants exist, but you might remember stories from your childhood about men riding dragonback. What if all of the old children's stories have bases in reality? Interesting to ponder."

I laughed. Usually, on the airship, I would cut Harkerpal off when he went off on his tangential storytelling. Now, it brought me comfort. It was nice to hear his voice again. "A fascinating story, Harkerpal," I said. "Have you looked into the ship's condition?"

Harkerpal frowned. "I'm afraid she sustained terrible damage. The angle at which the *Liliana* landed caused the forward turbine shaft to bend. We're going to have to fabricate a new one, plus a lot of woodwork to replace the bridge and the mess. Interestingly, outside of the gaping hole in the bottom of the ship and the structures atop the deck, the frame remained intact. We're going to need to conscript aether-fuel powered cranes to right her and see what else needs to be done. At least we won't have to build a new airship from scratch Ordinarily, I believe we could manage the repairs in a month, but with the city rebuilding efforts..." Harkerpal shook his head.

"Did anyone find a leather book? A journal in the ship?" I asked.

Harkerpal shook his head. "The area hasn't been completely excavated yet, however."

"Someone needs to tell King Malaky to get some people there. It's of utmost importance."

"Did somebody speak my name?" The king's voice boomed from down the hall. He stepped forward, along with a sizable retinue. The entourage included two palace guards, my father, Talyen and baby Lilly, James, Princess Reina, and Mr. du Gearsmith. All of them looked freshly bathed and dressed. I must have looked a wreck by comparison. I flushed with embarrassment.

"Hey, Zair-bear," James said with a wave. He had a leather vest on, a sword at his hip, and a pendant with the crest of Malaky on the right side of his chest. His face looked older than before, some smile lines showing. Something in his eyes seemed more like a man than before, for a lack of better way of describing it. When our eyes met, I didn't feel any awkwardness or embarrassment anymore. It wasn't odd. Whatever had pained us before had been resolved by the trials of war.

"Hi," I said. "This is quite the greeting committee."

"Intentionally so," King Malaky said. He motioned to Mr. du Gearsmith, who held a small wooden box in his hands. The latter man handed the box to the king, who then stepped toward my bedside.

I looked at everyone curiously, as they had coy, smiling faces returned to me. What in the world was going on?

"The doctors have had us avoid giving you updates the last few days, wishing us to leave you alone to rest. However, you should know that the Wyranth have been expelled from the northern half of Rislandia, and by all accounts, those who remain in the south are falling back," King Malaky said.

"The plan worked, Zaira," My father added. "We successfully gathered the bulk of the Wyranth's remaining forces into one place when they thought they could exterminate us once and for all. The anti-serum was very effective. The twenty-third regiment encountered small bands who weren't impacted by it, but every battle has been a rout so far. We are finally winning."

"There's still a lot of work to do," King Malaky said. "We'll discuss these matters later, but our priority will be to rebuild and ensure everyone in Rislandia has enough to eat when winter falls. Regardless, all of this can wait until tomorrow. Today, we celebrate."

I nodded, not exactly following where he was going with this.

King Malaky opened the wooden box and held it toward me. Inside was a pendant of gold and brass, the shape of a sword. "Baron Zaira von Monocle, I wish to present you with the Rislandia Kingdom's medal of valor for your efforts in fighting the Wyranth and saving the kingdom. Without your tenacity and creativity, I doubt we would be standing here today." He held the box toward me.

I picked up the medal. It was heavy, made of real gold from what I could tell of the soft metallic feel. It must have been worth a fortune. My heart sank suddenly, recalling how I'd met with the Iron Emperor and how some of this might have been avoided if it weren't for my foolishness. "I'm not sure I can accept. I—"

My father cleared his throat. "Zaira, I discussed the matter with King Malaky. We keep nothing from each other. We are both in agreement that under the circumstances, you did all you could do and acted in good faith for the kingdom. Whether matters could have been different if you had told us the full truth of what had occurred, no one can say. Events may have proceeded in the same manner. Without your expedition to Zenwey and return with Mr. Rhys to do such excellent work on the anti-serum, then we would have been completely overrun."

King Malaky nodded. "Your instincts were correct, Zaira. And I want to acknowledge that. Please, accept this token of Rislandia's gratitude toward you."

I looked between the two men, biting my lip. I still couldn't help but feel there were many more people deserving of this honor than I was, but I clutched the medal all the same, holding it to my chest. "I'll treasure this forever. Thank you." My eyes moistened. I couldn't hold the tears back and found them trickling down my cheek.

Mr. du Gearsmith stepped forward and handed me a ribbon with a clip so the medal could hang from it. "For public ceremonies, you should wear this around your neck. You're a hero of the people now, Baron von Monocle."

A hero. It sounded so odd. I didn't want to acknowledge it. I just did what anyone would have done in the situation. I wiped the tears from my eyes, and then took the ribbon, hooking the medal onto it, and then placing it around my neck. It felt heavy, but the others looked so happy to see it on me. "Thank you," I said again, unable to find other words.

King Malaky smiled. "It's you who has our thanks. If there's anything you require from this kingdom, you have my ear."

Silence fell across the room for a long moment as I considered. At this point, I knew I could ask for anything. Lands, titles, riches, fulfillment of dreams of most people. But I didn't want any of that. Even though it sounded pleasant to settle down somewhere with Ethan, start a family, I couldn't see myself in that life after I'd seen the whole world. Maybe later, but not right now. "The airship..." I said.

"We'll make sure she is back in working order as soon as possible. Given how the ship was integral to saving our kingdom, and how much of a symbol of fear it evokes in the Wyranth, it's imperative to get her back in the skies."

Harkerpal beamed with that answer.

"Is there anything else?" King Malaky asked, amusement on his face.

I glanced between everyone. I had everything I ever wanted here. My family, my friends. It would have been nice to have Ethan here as well, but he would return. There would be plenty of time to see him.

Still, something felt wrong. I worried about the journal with the airship designs. If it somehow fell into Wyranth hands...

No, this was a time to be positive. We'd driven the Wyranth back and restored the kingdom. I held my head up high and tried to put on my most professional countenance. "I only await further orders, your majesty."

ALSO BY JON DEL ARROZ

The Adventures Of Baron Von Monocle:
For Steam And Country
Knight Training
The Blood Of Giants
The Fight For Rislandia

The Stars Entwined

Gravity Of The Game

ABOUT THE AUTHOR

Jon Del Arroz is a #1 Amazon Bestselling author, "the leading Hispanic voice in science fiction" according to PJMedia.com, and winner of the 2018 CLFA Book Of The Year Award. As a contributor to *The Federalist*, he is also recognized as a popular journalist and cultural commentator. Del Arroz writes science fiction, steampunk, and comic books, and can be found most weekends in section 127 of the Oakland Coliseum cheering on the A's.

Twitter: @jondelarroz
Instagram: @jdelarroz
Website: delarroz.com
Email: jdaguestposts@gmail.com